BROKEN PARTS

PARTS OF ME SERIES, BOOK 3

J. A. WYNTERS

Broken Parts, Parts of Me series, Book 3

Editing by: Sarah Villanueva at Dear Jane Editing

Cover design: Jo- Anne Walker

Interior Formatting: Dawn Lucous, Yours Truly Book Services

You are about to continue on this journey spanning FIVE books. If you bought this ticket and are on board this freight train, prepare for it to be a long and bumpy ride as we delve into all the uncomfortable parts of life. These may trigger some readers so be sure you want to continue. These books will end on cliffhangers, have twists and turns and this train is sure to be derailed as it enters a long dark tunnel of depravity.

YOU HAVE BEEN WARNED.

Adult themes, strong language, graphic scenes. Enter at your own risk.

PART XVII

S imone is dead.
Gone.

I suddenly felt like an orphan; alone in the world, untethered, without roots, and in danger of floating away.

My heart ached in the way only sorrow could understand —bleak and dark and agonising. A piece of it would be forever carved out and buried alongside her.

Another piece of my heart, maybe the very last I had left to give.

I slammed the car door and walked.

How the fuck did I end up there?

I sucked in the autumn air. Heaped brown leaves decorated the dying grass—everything around me was falling, dying, breaking, or disappearing into hibernation. Autumn was the season that ended all others, sucking away life and warmth, light and colour. It ushered in the bleakness of winter, allowing it to creep in uninvited.

I wandered along the familiar path, my heavy legs leading my body as numbness gripped my insides —and there it was —that fucking bench.

I collapsed onto it. Maybe I was looking for comfort,

maybe I was needing some quiet, or maybe this place felt too much like home.

I sat staring blankly at the leaves as they rustled against one another in the breeze, clinging to the branches, holding on to the hope of living just one more day.

I felt it then, the warm trickle as it burned my skin. I wiped away the tear just as another leaked down my cheek and then another; and despite Salvatore's words ringing in my ears—*No emotion, no regret, no turning back*—I wanted to shove it all down, force it into the vault of memories and anguish I'd been carrying. Simone always said there was a storm inside of me, and she was right. Now that the grief had begun to spill, it was a tempest that would destroy everything in its path.

The grief pitched with each of my expelled breaths. The tears poured from me in a deluge that threatened to drown me in my own sorrow and to consume me entirely. They fell with a violence greater than any gale, wracking sobs that tore through me in waves of wretchedness until all that remained was an all-consuming emptiness.

The gnawing hollowness allowed for the anger to rise, to fill up the gaping hole left by this new loss. It rose slowly, a low simmering fire that grew and bubbled over like a volcano. It spilled into every part of me, filling me with cold fury.

I sat until I shook, full of hatred and anger until I was full to the brim—no longer empty, no longer hollow. I tore from the bench, returning to my car and slid into the driver's seat. My bitterness leaked from me, stuffing the car with heat, brewing a storm cloud against the gloomy skies.

Simone was dead and Emilio Rocco was going to follow her into the grave. But no one would mourn for him.

By the time I arrived back at The Hill, my knuckles were white. My grip threatened to tear the steering wheel from its place.

I smashed through the door into Sin, coming through the hidden back door. The likes of me were still unwelcome in an establishment such as this. I bet all those fuckers spending their money and hiding from their wives would shed a few kilos in sweat if they knew I owned this hotel.

I found Romeo lurking in the shadows; he had the smile on his face that men get when they see a pair of tits. Their brain mostly switches off and their bodies react; they long and ache and need to stick themselves somewhere tight and warm.

I rushed over to him, pushing him along the wall. His back bounced against it with a thud, and he flinched at the sight of my face, "Where the fuck is Mia?"

"Salvatore let her upstairs." He stammered.

I nodded, "Where did she go today?"

Romeo's eyes flicked away from me and his fingers twitched at his sides, "I don't know?"

I wanted to pin him to the wall with my hand around his throat and smash his head so far into the plaster that he would disappear into it. But there were people around— paying customers. I clenched my teeth and hissed, "What do you mean you don't know?"

Romeo's restless gaze swung back and forth avoiding mine, "She gave me the slip."

"Would you like to say that again slowly?"

He cleared his throat, "I erm…lost her…for just a while."

I inched closed, my larger body closing over him, "What the fuck does that mean?"

He rubbed the back of his neck, "It means she went into a ladies shop, and I didn't want to follow her in there. You now, stick out like a sore thumb? And well, she never came out. When I went to look for her, she was gone."

"What were your orders?"

"To follow Mia."

I eyed him.

"Wherever she went." He mumbled the rest like a scared school boy.

"And did you?"

"I tried. I mean…"

I raised my hand and he flinched away, the back of his head meeting the wall with bang.

"I'm sorry boss, it won't happen again."

"How long?"

"Boss?"

"How. Long. Was. She. Gone?" I hissed the words through gritted teeth.

"About three hours." He cleared his throat again, trying to become one with the wall.

My fists clenched at my sides, my eyes bored into his for a few moments more, "This conversation is not over. Find Salvatore, we have work to do." I backed away and turned towards my private elevator.

The walls closed in around me as it rose upwards. Flames of anger and confusion licked at my skin, beckoning me to burn and destroy everything and everyone.

I stalked out of the elevator and found Mia sitting on the couch. Her short shorts peeked from below her long, black t-shirt, her hair cascaded down her shoulders—wild and untamed—and her long legs were crossed over as she stretched across the couch with a book in her hand.

All my anger had turned to white fury, an iceberg—worried and desperate below the surface of the choppy water above.

"Where the fuck have you been?" My voice was cold and her shoulders stiffened at my demeanour.

"I went shopping." She huffed at me, her forehead creasing.

"And lost Romeo in the process."

"Not my fault he couldn't keep up." She shrugged and the

casualness of her answer fanned the flames that burned inside me.

"Couldn't keep up?"

She shrugged again and it took all of my will not to erupt into a menacing beast. I grabbed the book from her hand and flung it across the room.

"Hey—" She started, but I was on top of her. My hands pinned hers above her head, my face an inch from hers.

"Simone is dead, your apartment was ransacked and you were kidnapped. I am trying to keep you safe, and you just go off and disappear?"

"Simone is dead?" Her eyes grew wide and her mouth fell.

I ignored her, "Where the fuck did you go Mia?"

"Gabriel you're hurting me."

"Where?"

"I just went shopping."

"The truth," My grip tightened around her wrists as the grip on my sanity slipped away.

"I just wanted to get something—a surprise."

"And that took three hours?" I growled.

"It does when you have eyes all around town and everyone reports back to you."

I released her hands and leaned my forehead into hers.

"Gabriel?"

"I can't protect you if I don't know where you are. I can't lose you Mia, not you too."

I felt the surge of sadness as it crashed through me like a tsunami. The tears welled in my eyes and fell onto Mia's face, they rolled over the side even as her own eyes watered.

"It's ok Gabriel." Her thin arms wrapped themselves around me, giving me permission to fall apart, allowing me to be vulnerable and broken—to shed tears, to shed skin, to prepare for war. "It's ok, it will all be over soon."

Of course she was right, but there would be so much more pain before it did.

PART XVIII

"Wake up." Simone's face was tight, crowfeet puling at the edges, green flames burning coolly behind her fierce eyes.

"Wake up Gabriel," she shook me again and I uncurled, my body aching from another night on the floor. Spots whimpered beside me and I reached for him.

"It's ok buddy, go back to sleep."

"You can't keep sleeping here." My body tightened at her words, and I sat up looking at her face.

"I told you, as long as Spots is here, I'm not leaving." We locked eyes, I'd hoped she heard the threat in my tone. She ignored me.

"I didn't say you couldn't stay. I said you can't sleep here anymore, on the floor, in the cold. I will arrange for something more suitable for a…" she appraised me for a moment, "a man your age."

"Oh right."

"Now get up and get yourself cleaned up, it's breakfast time."

I nodded, stretching my aching muscles but, despite my

attempts, the tension remained winding me up tight like a spring. In the last two weeks I had watched Tony die, lost Rita, murdered a Judge and seen my best friend get hurt. I was anything but ok.

I made my way to the toilet and washed my face in the basin. I looked almost as shit as I felt, dishevelled hair and dark rings under my eyes, but I was too worried about Spots to worry about myself. Now that I had Tony's files, I had a job to do. I had vowed to cleanse the souls of those children by burning those of their fathers, and that was what I intended on doing.

When I walked out, the lights were on and a cacophony of sounds greeted me. Simone was dressed in green overalls with her Paw Prints Rescue logo embroidered over her left breast. Her hair was pulled back in a messy ponytail and light, white-blonde hair twirled around as she moved.

"Right, well time to make yourself useful then," she pointed at a large green bin, "Grab that and start scooping. One scoop for the little dogs, two for the medium, three for the large."

I stared at her and swung my gaze to the bin. This was not what I envisioned when she said breakfast; but as I started scoping dried food and distributing it into bowls and feeding all the dogs, I felt comfort—something akin to usefulness. For a short time, my mind was pulled away from the numbers that haunted me.

One dead boss.

One dead friend.

Two long weeks of watching Spots suffer in pain.

Seventy-three children—children whose fear and pain had been forever captured on polaroids, whose hunted expressions where inked into my brain.

Seven hundred and two videos—crimes, weights on my shoulders.

Numbers, so many numbers. Now, I only had to think about three.

One scoop for the small dogs, two for the medium dogs, and three for the big dogs. One, two, three. It was easy, simple, and refreshing.

When we were done with feeding the animals, Simone invited me upstairs. The wooden staircase— once painted black—showed its age, chipped and worn by years of ascending and descending. She pushed a green door open and we entered her apartment.

It smelt different than the floor below; the sterile hospital-grade smell had become more neutral, more fragrant, but the smell of wet dog followed us everywhere.

Two outdated, floral couches sat atop a tattered, lined carpet platted together with every colour of the rainbow. She led me through the cluttered lounge housing boxes of dog food, towers of folded towels that leaned precariously against one another, bottles of dog shampoo, and laundry detergent. Framed pictures of dogs covered every available surface. The back of the door was decorated with leashes hanging like a mismatched bead door curtain.

On the wall, an oversized picture hung, mounted in a decorative white frame. In it, two men stood on either side of a woman, she wore a white shirt and her youth and joy spilt out of the picture. The two men looked almost identical, except the one on the right had a day's worth of growth on his chin, while the other looked about my age. He had the same eyes as the woman, green and intelligent. They were all mid laughter, a perfectly captured moment frozen forever in time—a beautiful happy moment.

I wondered what happened to the men in the picture.

The round dining room table was barren, as if an invisible barrier stopped the clutter from spilling over from one room to the next. The cheap plastic table was covered in a see-through plastic sheet, and two foldout plastic chairs sat around it. It almost didn't surprise me. Simone stepped into the small kitchenette and gestured that I sit at the table. I obliged as she tinkered about, opening and closing decade old cupboards.

"Coffee?" She studied me as if trying to figure out if I was old enough to drink the stuff.

"Yes, please." I cocked my head at her and she nodded to herself then pottered around the kitchen pulling out plates, cups, knives, and teaspoons.

She placed two steaming cups of coffee on the table and came back with two plates heaped with toast. She grabbed some jam, marmalade, and butter from the fridge, and went back for a jar of peanut butter. Once she had placed everything on the table she sat and gestured, "Help yourself."

As if on cue, my stomach grumbled and I grabbed a piece of toast, lathering it with strawberry jam. I stuffed the toast into my mouth and suddenly I felt like that nine-year-old boy Alice sold to Tony—the one that Salvatore fed.

I shovelled three more slices of toast into my mouth and washed them down with coffee. It was too weak and tasted too much like sugared water, but I didn't complain.

"Thank you." I licked my fingers clean and sipped on the obnoxious drink.

"When was the last time you ate?"

Two days.

"I don't remember." I lied. It didn't matter, the truth was that some habits died hard. I could've been starving or this could've been my third meal of the day. When it came to food, it went down as quickly as I saw it. I learned early on that it was me or them. If it wasn't going into my mouth, it would go into someone else's.

Simone just nodded and hugged her mug, holding it close to her mouth and blowing. The steam rose up like a veil over her green eyes.

"How old are you Gabriel?"

"Twenty." I straightened my back and sat against the chair as if my posture gave weight to my age.

Her mouth stretched into a thin line before she started talking again, "Your friend from the other night was very…serious."

"Salvatore? He's harmless."

"Is he? "

I shrugged.

"Are all your friends that serious?" I knew what she was asking.

"Some more than others I guess."

"And these friends of yours, would they be coming to look for you? Here?"

"No one knows I'm here—no one but Salvatore, and he's not a big talker. It's why we get on so well." I hoped she'd take the hint.

"What kind of trouble are you in Gabriel?"

"Nothing too serious." I tried to shrug off her question, but her eyes bore into me.

She put her mug down and sighed, "If you don't want to tell me, that's fine as long as you understand two things: my dogs come first and if any harm comes to any of them because you're here, there will hell to pay." She stared directly into my eyes, waiting for me to acknowledge her statement.

I tipped my head and she continued.

"Secondly, you earn your keep here. You don't just get to sit around all day."

"I can pay you."

"I don't want your money."

"Why?"

"It's no good here."

"Looks like you could use it." My gaze swung across the room, I regretted the words as soon as they were out of my mouth.

Her lips twitched but she ignored my words and sighed instead, "I've dealt with a lot of strays in my life. Some can be trained; they will always be loyal and good—a bit like your Spots, I suspect." She scrutinised me as she spoke, "While others can never be broken, they're just too damaged. You can keep them contained and give them love; and when they're busy, they forget about their troubles and wag their tails and keep a distance," her eyes clung to my face, "But despite appearances—whether they seem loyal or damaged—there's always a chance that one day they'll turn on you and bite. Because in their very core, they are an animal, a predator, a thing made for hunting and killing. The trick is to keep them busy so they forget."

"In your little story, which one am I?"

"I guess we will find out soon enough, won't we?" With that she placed her cup in the sink and left her toast uneaten, "Work starts in twenty minutes."

"What about Spots? I won't leave him."

"He will be downstairs all day, same as you. He isn't going anywhere anytime soon," she walked over to the door, "You can sit with him during your breaks." She left me in her apartment, her light steps echoing in the narrow staircase.

I sat for a few more moments digesting her words and her insipid coffee, then got up to walk out. I stopped in front of the picture, feeling its pull. The people in that picture looked like they knew happiness once. I wondered what it felt like—to experience so much joy with people that love you. I unglued my eyes from the photo and shook away the thoughts. I scrambled downstairs and found Simone in the cramped, half-empty storeroom.

"Is that you in that picture?"

"Yes."

"And the men?"

"My husband and son." Her breath hitched a little but she

didn't look up as she spoke, pulling clean towels from a shelf and piling them into her lap.

"Where is he now, your son?"

She stopped and looked into my eyes, her mouth slanted to the ground, "He went off to fight a war that had nothing to do with him, and he never came back." Her voice was bitter.

"He was trying to do the right thing."

"And see where that landed him."

"Someone has to go to war. Someone has to face the ugliness to preserve the beauty in this world." I don't know why I felt the need to defend a man I'd never met or knew anything about—but as heat flooded my veins and my heart thumped faster—I wondered if it was really him I was trying to defend.

"Maybe." She sighed and went back to her towels.

That first day I learned a few valuable lessons, lessons that I never forgot, lessons that saved my life.

Simone approached one of the pens and four excited dogs jumped up and reared. Happy to see her, their tails wagged and their barks and howls echoed through the space.

"Calm down you lot, I'm just here for Frankie. Come on Frankie, come here boy." She called to a larger dog with long golden fur. She reached for his nape and guided him out of the pen while pushing the door closed.

"Hi Frankie, this is Gabriel." She smiled at the dog.

The dog came up to me and sniffed around, his tail wagging.

"Right, come this way you two."

She led us down the corridor and into a room with a giant steel basin and taps, "Time for a bath Frankie, you're going to a new home today." She beamed at the prospect.

"Get him in the basin." She directed me.

"How?"

Simone ignored my question, pretending she didn't hear me.

I inhaled, exhaled then called for the dog, "Hey Frankie come here, get in the basin." The dog approached me sniffed, then ran circles around me, barking and wagging his tail. "Oh come on buddy, get in." I moved towards the basin and tapped the steel. The dog ignored me and Simone's lips twitched.

"Hey Frankie, I'll give you a biscuit if you get in the bath."

"No!" Simone cut me off, "Never bribe a dog. Don't encourage bad behaviour and bad habits. If he comes to accept a treat each time he is asked to do something, he will only respond to bribes. Find another way."

I took a deep breath, brushing away my failure and tried again. "Frankie, come here boy, come on." The dog continued to ignore me.

Simone rolled her eyes and walked to the basin, "Frankie sit!" It was a short, sharp demand and the dog responded immediately. "Come here!" He stood up and jumped into the basin, allowing Simone to hook a leash that was attached on the wall.

"Good boy Frankie." She gushed at the dog, patted his head then grabbed the hose, saturating his thick fur. Frankie tipped his head, allowing Simone to scrub and scratch shampoo into his golden fur that pulled away from his body like a curtain. His tail wagged as she washed him. Rinsing away the white bubbles, we all watched them drain away into the sink like the futures none of us envisioned having.

"Gabriel pass me the drier hose please."

I stepped behind Simone—the narrow berth forcing me to squeeze myself between the wall and her—I placed a hand on her shoulder to keep my balance. At my movement, Frankie bared his teeth and growled, his eyes locked onto mine.

"Gabriel, look down and take a step back."

I did as she said. "It's ok Frankie," she cooed the dog, "Gabriel was helping me, don't worry. He's a friend."

The dog seemed to visibly relax, his tail wagged again as Simone dried him, brushing through his fur, grooming him for his new owners. I stood aside and watched as flurries of fur blew through the air like snow.

When she was done, she brushed his fur once more and allowed him to jump up and lick her hand. She giggled and pulled him to her, "Oh, there's a pretty, clean boy. Ready to go." She scratched behind his ears and led him back to the main hall where she put him in his own pen.

"Why did he snap at me before? He seemed so friendly."

"Frankie is very friendly, but he thought I was in danger. He was protecting me. I had to show him that I was in control of the situation and I didn't need his help just then."

"But I wasn't aggressive."

"That's not the point," Simone folded her arms across her chest. "At their core, dogs are wolves—hunters, protectors—and that primal need to protect the pack will always be their most important. When you own a dog, you need to always be the alpha. Assert yourself, remind them that they are dogs, that you are the one in charge or they'll always run circles around you."

I waited for her to finish.

"Even the most loyal and friendliest of dogs can bite."

I never forgot her lesson, not really. I just didn't pay as much attention as I should have.

The rest of that day I spent between Spots, cleaning dogs and dog shit, feeding, cleaning and stocking Simone's meagre shelfs.

When Frankie's new family came to collect him, she smiled and laughed and scratched his head one final time.

When they had gone, I could see tears brimming in her eyes.

"Why don't you have your own dog?"

"I do." She gestured with her hands to the pens.

I cocked my head, "None of them are yours."

"They're all mine." She stated matter of factly.

"But you give them all away…"

She sighed a little and scanned the room, looking over the dogs, serenity spreading across her features, "I have known love—deep, affectionate love—from someone who belonged to me, and when he was gone, he buried a piece of me with him." Her mouth turned in a melancholy smile, "I rent love now. It comes in waves of wagging tails and slobber. I don't get too attached, that way my heart can never really be broken."

"You're lying."

"Excuse me?"

"You don't just cry over dogs you're not attached to."

Her mouth tipped upwards and she scrutinised me for a long minute. "It's a passing love, and it's not forever. I get all I need from them."

"Do you?"

She turned away and left me to finish sweeping the floor. She never did answer my question and, in the end, she did get attached. Spots and I found that empty spot in her heart and, whether or not she'd ever admit it, I know that we filled it just as she filled ours.

It was the first in many such days—animals and Simone and sleeping next to Spots.

It took Simone two weeks to allow me into her apartment.

The thing that Simone never understood was that she never *just* gave me shelter and a place to hide, she had given me a home. She gave me comfort and the benefit of the doubt. Yes I had to work, earn my place, gain her trust, but I also got respect and left alone.

She allowed me time with Spots, allowed me to nurture him back to health as I stayed hidden behind her shelter walls and planned my revenge, my retribution, and my reckoning. When I was ready, I unleashed it like the devil.

T he funeral was beautiful— as beautiful as a thing could be when you have to put a body in the ground. I've buried many bodies in my life. Most have been in shallow graves or endless voids, nameless ditches that will never be found. Simone was going to be remembered if it was the last thing I could do for her.

The heavy wooden casket lowered into the ground and lay there, keeping her safe and warm beneath six feet of dirt.

I didn't shed any tears and didn't give a eulogy. I left that to Alex and the other stooges. I'd already said my goodbyes, I'd already spent my tears. All that was left was an empty void that I needed to carve out. I needed to fashion the right knife for the job, and only cold seeding revenge would cut out my new wound.

As we left the cemetery, I caught a glimpse of Alice. She had crawled out of her hole and come to pay her respects; or maybe she wanted to ensure the woman I had thought of as my mother was dead. Maybe she wanted her place in my heart back. I had thrown dirt into the rabbit hole that held the feelings I had for Alice; I wasn't going to let her dig them out—not today of all days.

She waved to me but I ignored her. I walked straight to the waiting car and ushered Mia inside. I saw the questioning look she gave me, but Mia knew better than to say anything. We drove back to The Hill in silence.

We stepped into the penthouse, lights twinkled below us. On any other night it would have been beautiful, but tonight the shine had worn off and the world felt a little tarnished— dirty even.

Mia looked beautiful in a black dress that hugged her figure, her face was drawn and her eyes rimmed red.

I don't know why she was crying, maybe it was for me.

"It was a beautiful service."

"Sure." I shrugged, not sure what else there was to say. I discarded my jacket, threw it across the couch and unbuttoned my shirt. I let it fall open, and Mia's greedy eyes took me in.

She stepped closer, her delicate hand falling on my chest.

"How are you holding up Gabriel?"

"I don't want to talk about it." Her hand lingered on my chest, and her eyes burned into mine.

"Poor, broken Gabriel," she whispered, her warm breath on my chest as her lips graze my skin, "Let me make it better for you, let me take your pain away."

"You want to take my pain away? How?" I pushed her away, not in the mood for her games.

"Let me make it…"

"Better?" I crept forward, and she retreated as I stalked forward.

"Better? Can you bring the dead back to life? Can you take this pain away, this emptiness? Can you make this guilt sting less, hurt less?" With each question, I took another step forward forcing her backwards into the room.

"Gabriel I…"

"No, no more empty words! I said I don't want to talk about it." There was nowhere left to go, and my body pinned hers to the floor-to-ceiling window, lights glaring at us from below.

"Who said anything about talking? Let me *make* it better."

Mia pushed up on her tiptoes and her lips grazed mine, her eyes dark and tender.

"Mia…"

She pushed up again taking my lip in hers, sucking the pain from me.

I growled at the intrusion, at her demand to pierce through my feelings and her desire to make my heart spill its guts and bleed all over the posh penthouse.

I gripped her arm then spun her body, twisting her hand and pinning it against her back. She moaned as i tightened my grip and pushed her body against the window.

"You want to make it better?" I growled in her ear even as I unbuckled my belt, "You want to feel how I feel?"

She whimpered against the window, her ass pushing against my growing erection.

I shoved my pants and underwear off in a swift move and flung her dress up, yanking her underwear to the side. I plunged into her, not waiting for permission. I wanted to give her what she'd asked for, all the pain and anguish. I drove it into her in brutal thrusts and she ground against me, taking it all. I ploughed my guilt and anger into her at a punishing pace, and she whimpered my name against the cold window, her breath materialising on the pane.

I poured my anger into her, all of my devastation and—with a final, brutal, splintering stroke—all of my sadness spilled into her. Mia screamed for me or maybe because of me or maybe because she felt it all. Deep down our hearts broke together in one shattering moment, and all the lights exploded behind my eyes in stardust.

M ia was sleeping—a restful, beautiful sleep. I guess those with a guilt-free conscious really do sleep well.

She hadn't said anything when I pulled away from her and left her against the window; there was only silence between us.

I stationed Romeo at the base of the elevator and told him

not to let her out of his sight. He gave me a nervous nod and I left.

I carved the dark night with my headlights as I drove home. Maybe because I knew I would never go past there again, I ended up at 'Paw Prints Rescue'—or what was left of it. The car sat idle as I stared at the gaping hole. The tall building that once stood there was now a pile of blackened columns and broken bricks set on powdered ash and scorched ground.

I stepped out, ducking under the worn crime scene tape and moved towards the wreckage, my feet propelling me forward and my body aching with loss.

In the darkness I drew pictures in my mind, building flesh on the skeleton that remained. I Conjured the dog pens, the office, and the storage room. My gaze shifted to the stairs; they had crumbled with the walls and only the bottom two remained, blackened and charred. I sifted through the remains of Simone's beloved shelter. Paper turned to ash in my hands, coating my shoes and fingers in black dust. Nothing was left of her, just a memory that will fade once those who knew her die. I hoped she didn't see the dogs suffer. That would have scorched her heart in a way the fire never could. I turned away, not looking back.

This was my final goodbye.

The lights exploded to life, and I sucked in the smell of oil and gasoline. The work floor stood empty; the boys would be back in the morning, customers would bring their cars, and life would go on.

I exhaled and walked over to the corner where I pulled away the plastic sheet and stared at the Harley. She was stunning with a finished chrome coat and new seat. I grabbed the guard and bolted it on, making sure not to hit the fender. As

I tightened the final screws, I felt lighter. This day has been a long time coming; too many delays and too many deaths stood in my way, but tonight I would resurrect one thing from the dead.

My heart slammed in my chest and my breathing became heavier as my elation grew and expanded. I sucked in a deep breath, feeling a vortex of emotion inside of me that desperately searched for a way out—building underneath my skin, gusting between sinew and muscle, raging inside my veins, propelling my blood, and driving into my blustering heart as I exhale.

There was only one way to hone in on that feeling, to release all the tension and hold on to that moment: I had to ride her.

I filled her up with oil and petrol, and slid the key into the ignition. Anticipation crawled along my skin like a chill.

My heart leapt into my throat as I climbed onto the leather seat and allowed myself to settle into it, my weight shifting as it sank into the contoured softness. I slammed my eyes shut and turned her on, listening—every muscle on edge, every nerve end alight.

The engine roared to life, the sound blew through me like a hurricane and shook me to my core. She sounded like a caged beast that's been set free. I listened to her roar and waited until, at last, the angry sound settled into a low purr. My face split open into a smile as the engine purred and fell into a dimmed hum, as the oil spread through the engine, lubricating the cold steal, and bringing her to life. She was content, singing to me.

I revved the engine and felt life reverberating beneath my skin, crawling along my veins and flowing through my body —it was beautiful. The feeling was warm and silky, like something resembling happiness. The wild animal below me urging it on with its purrs, begging to be set free.

I flipped the switch and the roller door came to life,

lifting slowly and letting in the darkness from outside. It called to me—beckoning— and I answered its call.

I opened the throttle and the garage was behind me in seconds. I could already feel my anxiety shed like old skin. The Harley tore down the road, screaming as it sliced the dark night with a wild screech of freedom. The road blurred beneath me as I forced the bike faster. The wind wrapped itself around me, pushing its way beneath my clothes and into my nose, carrying with it a unique concoction of acrid exhaust pipes, smoke, spicy perfume, and humanity in all its odorous depravity and glory. Every nuance of it stuffed deeper into my nose and I sucked it all in as I opened up the throttle more.

The world poured into my eyes without limitations— lights, buildings, objects—I became hyperaware of everything around me. All of my senses tingled as if my nervous system had been shocked and awoken after a long, numbing slumber.

I rode.

I rode until buildings disappeared and the side of the road became flatter, darker, and rounder. My skin prickled with the chill as the temperature dropped, and I smiled knowing I was out of the city and free.

The faster I cruised, the thicker the air became. It whistled in my ears and stroked my hair; it wrapped itself around me, no longer stale and sour but free and fresh. My mind shed away its burdens, the worry and fear fell away like dying stars in the sky. The bike tore a smile out of me that stretched and grew and expanded as I tore down the road.

In truth, I never wanted to turn back. I should've kept going. I should have sped on into the night, ripping the memories of this day from my skin and never look back.

But I was hooked. Like a fish on the end of the rod, Mia had caught me and my heart chugged for her, beating faster at the thought of never seeing her again. My body coiled at the idea, and the bike reared and wavered and tightened with my body.

I smashed on the break and the bike skidded to a screeching halt, leaving behind a long black scar on the road.

I looked ahead, the beam from the Harley slicing the road ahead. The bike had always been the bolt cutter to my past, the thing that was going to take me away from everything. There was nothing down that path; it was clear, guided by pure yellow light. There was no history there, no names, no books—a clean slate, a new beginning.

Behind me, just beyond the empty darkness, I could make out the twinkling lights of the city. A city where Mia slept in my penthouse alone, where Salvatore poured over lists, where Simone was six feet under, and where Alice was…who the fuck knew where she was.

My heart pounded as it rippled in my chest.

Forwards.

Backwards.

Fresh start.

Bad memories.

New beginnings.

Mia.

Mia.

Mia, it pounded—and I had my answer. Her line reeled me in, hooked tightly into me. I revved the engine, drowning in its rawness, in its powerful song and turned around and headed back to my garage. My future.

I slowed as I approached the garage, noticing a familiar car parked across the road. I pulled up to it and knocked on the window, the bike purring beneath me.

Romeo sat up, startled, and wound down his window.

"What are you doing here?"

"Mia is inside." I cocked a quizzical eyebrow at him. "She insisted. You said not to leave her side…"

I turned the bike towards the roller door and pulled away,

even as he kept talking. I smirked inside my helmet. Romeo didn't have to explain, that woman had a stubborn streak that would never break.

I rolled the bike into the workshop; Mia was sitting on a plastic chair she must have dragged in from the kitchen. One leg crossed over the other, and her hands folded across her chest. Her expression vacant.

I turned off the engine, listening to the ticking of the hot exhaust and brake discs as they cool until silence fell across the room. I climbed off the Harley, my body instantly missing the feel of the machine beneath me, the joy of the vibrations as they rang through me.

"I thought I'd find you here." She stood up seeming uncertain.

"Why did you come here?"

"I hate sleeping without you."

I wrenched a hand through my hair and shrugged.

"Ask Romeo to take you back to The Hill."

"No."

I looked at Mia and scrubbed my hands over my face, "Mia…"

"Will you be back?"

"Yes."

"Tonight?" I looked outside, the sun would soon rise and splash the horizon in purples and blues.

"Not much night left."

"Gabriel?"

"Probably not."

Her lips smacked together and stretched across her face in a thin line. She nodded and I could see the thoughts ticking behind her concerned eyes.

"I just need time."

"How much time?"

I scrubbed a hand over my face. It felt good to be wanted, needed; but what *I* needed was to be left alone. I've been alone for so long that I didn't know how to share my misery or my joy—all of me. I just shrugged.

"Ok." She gave me a wane smile.

"Ok?" I frowned.

"Why do you sound so surprised?"

"Because you are the most stubborn person I know. You never give in this easily, I was expecting more of a fight on my hands. "

Her mouth tilted slightly at my words and for a second I regretted them, fearing the argument I was expecting was about to happen.

"I can see how much pain you're in Gabriel."

"Thanks, luce mia." I smiled and snaked my hands around her waist my forehead leaning against hers. "Here you go doing that again."

"Doing what?"

"Making me smile when there's nothing to smile about."

"There's lots to smile about."

"Yeah? Like what?"

"We are here—together."

"Together?"

"I'm here for you, with you, and that's how it's always going to be."

Her words ignited the room and suddenly it was alight. "Always?"

"Always." Her eyes were fierce as they locked onto mine.

"Always is a very long time." I whispered against her lips.

"It's not long enough."

My mouth found hers, teasing her lips apart. I pulled her into me as I sank deeper into the kiss. A rush of helplessness overtook me. I yielded to her warmth, my need, her kindness and drowned in her affection.

I released her, breathless, dizzy, elated.

"I better go." She licked her glistening lips, her eyes wide.

I almost protested.

Almost.

Instead, I lead her to the car and opened the door. She climbed into the backseat and gave me a final wistful look.

"Make sure you get her back to The Hill. No stopovers. Follow her to the elevator and make sure she doesn't leave."

Romeo gave me a two-finger salute and took off into the breaking dawn.

PART XIX

I woke up covered in sweat; the dream had returned. It was the same, but different. It was changing, augmenting, twisting and, like so much around me, I couldn't control it.

I pushed away from Mia, who grumbled as I climbed out off the bed. I walked to the kitchen and made coffee. Fingers of light pushed away at the darkness and I watched the world wake up from my high-rise, wishing I was somewhere else.

I turned around when I saw Mia shuffle into the room, a grin on her face. She wore one of my T-shirts, it swallowed her whole and fell across her shoulder exposing the long lines of her neck. She looked delectable.

"What are you smiling at?"

"I'm just enjoying the view."

"Oh?"

She closed the distance between us and landed a soft peck on my lips and grabbed my coffee from my hand, taking a sip. "Mmmm, morning."

Her lip twitched as she looked at me from beneath her long lashes, taking another long sip from my coffee.

I chuckled at her antics and returned to the kitchen to make myself a new cup. I watched the dark liquid fill the cup and wondered when things had become so comfortable between us. I watched Mia drinking my coffee, beaming at me. My heart skipped a beat.

"Would you like some breakfast? I can order some."

"Sure, what does one eat on her first day of being thirty?" She stretched an arm over head as if she didn't just drop a blatant bomb.

"Why didn't you tell me?"

"I just did." She smiled the sly devilish smile of hers, and my cock twitched.

"Mia." I warned her.

"With Simone and everything else that's been happening…"

"That still doesn't mean you get to miss your birthday!" I dragged my hand through my hair, my mind racing at a hundred miles a minute.

"Get dressed, we're going out for breakfast."

"Gabriel…"

"I said go get ready."

"Gabriel, seriously—"

"If you question me one more time, I'll not be held accountable for what happens."

At that she paused and sighed, "I'm going, I'm going."

A minute later the shower came to life and I grabbed the phone. Salvatore first, then the rest. I was going to make sure Mia never forgot her thirtieth birthday.

She chose pancakes with vanilla ice cream and chocolate sauce. I was mesmerised as she licked her sweet lips and tucked her hair behind her ears, how she smiled and laughed and talked as if it's always been us. Something rumbled inside of me, my body quaked like tectonic plates moved beneath the surface, shifting rearranging, creating new worlds. I knew just then how I felt, how I would always feel about Mia and it scared me more than anything else ever had.

When we approached the The Hill, I wrapped my hand around her shoulder and pulled her closer to me.

"There's a surprise waiting for you upstairs, I want you to enjoy it."

She gave me a bewildered look that made me chuckle.

"A surprise? You didn't have to."

"I know, but I wanted to. I want to make today special for you."

"I don't need special, I just need you."

My heart constricted with her words and my lips brushed hers, "And you'll have me," I smiled at her, "But you'll also get taken care of."

She gasped, "What does that mean?"

"Patience."

Her face furrowed and she folded her hands across her chest. Patience was not one of her virtues, and I was totally ok with that.

When we arrived, I led her to the elevator and punched in the code.

I kissed her cheek gently, "Enjoy."

"You're not coming?" She pouted.

"Just a few things to organise and I'll be up."

She sucked on her lower lip and nodded, finally stepping into the elevator. The door shut behind her and heat tugged at my chest. There was so much I wanted to do for her, give her. She had become my everything.

I stepped into my office and found Salvatore going through old files and paperwork. He didn't look up as I walked in.

"Boss."

I ground my teeth and glared at him, "What've you found?"

"Still nothing. I am crossing names off the list and revisiting properties, but it's taking time."

"It's taking *too much* time."

At that, he shot me a look that was both wounded and annoyed. He looked tired in a way that I've never seen in him, he wore his guilt like a coat.

"I know." He let the papers drop to the desk and he slumped back into the chair, deflated.

"I'll be gone this weekend. Can you handle things?"

He cocked and eyebrow at me.

"Things have not been…as usual."

"I'll be fine." He straightened up in the chair and pulled on his jacket.

"If you're sure—"

"I've already made your reservations, it's all set. Go."

"It's just one night," our eyes locked. "Don't say it."

"I wasn't going to say a thing." He held his hands up in surrender.

I inhaled as I scanned the papers on my desk, "Maybe it's time to shake the tree and see what falls out?"

Salvatore's jaw locked as his eyes narrowed. "Lupe?"

"We got nothing to lose."

"We got everything to lose."

"We still have their videos."

"But if we bring them into this, they'll think there's a weakness. That's all they need, an excuse."

I rubbed my hands over my face and nodded, "I'll think about it tonight."

"Doubt it…" Salvatore mumbled, and I shot him a look that silenced him. Although, maybe we both knew he was right.

"You know," he rubbed his hand over his chin, where day old growth peppered his usually immaculate face, "You don't have to come back."

My heart tripped on his words and an eyebrow shot up.

Salvatore leaned forward onto the table, "You don't. You have all the money in the world, a few successful legitimate businesses, relative peace and a woman that can stand the sight of you." The tip of his mouth tilted upwards, "You don't need to come back."

I raked a hand through my hair and studied Salvatore, my lips pinched, "I *was* away, and you called me back."

"Gabriel—"

"I know. But until I find the fucker that took Mia and murdered Simone, I'm not going anywhere." My tone held a note of finality, and Salvatore tipped his head and pushed up from the chair. He grabbed a handful of papers and started scanning the list.

His gaze flicked to me, "Go. I have work to do."

With that, I left the office. I meandered around packed chairs, bikini clad waitresses and dancers who swung on poles, putting their bodies on display. I left Sin behind and went to my private elevator.

Mia was waiting upstairs, and I couldn't wait to see her.

The elevator chimed my arrival, and I stepped into my penthouse. I removed my shoes and stepped silently into the living area.

Mia lay face up on the table. Her brow furrowed, her mouth in a delectable pout as the masseuse kneaded her skin. She hovered that thin line between pleasure and pain. Her naked torso covered in a pristine white towel that sat just above the knees. The oil gleamed on her body, making her skin glow against the sun filtering through the windows.

I stole into the room and sat on the edge of the couch. I was a spectator to beauty.

I watched Mia as the black woman massaged her neck and shoulders, the folds of her skin gathering around the woman's expert fingers. Mia purred and winced as the woman elicited delectable moans from her. Mia's body stiffened and relaxed as she treaded a familiar line of pleasure and pain; the pleasure of being touched and healed, the pain of the muscle being pushed and prodded. The woman played her like a piano—ivory and ebony—drawing beautiful melodies from Mia that made my cock hard and needy. I wanted to devour her, to worship her, and to show her who I really was.

I crept over to the massage table and wordlessly signalled for the masseuse to leave. She lifted her hands from Mia and walked out of the room silently.

My hands glided over her slippery, warm shoulders, and she gasped as my strong hands gripped her skin and her eyes shot open. Her head lifted from the bed.

"Stay." I growled in her ear and her body quivered beneath me as she settled back into the bed.

Mia purred for me as I kneaded and teased her, following the contours of her shoulders and along her beautiful neck, down towards her chest. I peeled the towel from her, revealing her bare body. Mine hardened as hers softened beneath my touch.

I traced her body up and down again and again with slow, deep, long-flowing strokes, teasingly caressing her. She moaned and hissed under my touch, her body writhing beneath my hands. Her nipples hardening, her legs squirming and pressing together, sucking her lower lip into her mouth with soft moans. Her breath shallow, her chest rising up and down in quick succession. She looked anything but relaxed. I smirked at the sight of her.

"Turn over Mia." I ordered through clenched jaws. My self-control was dwindling with every brush of her skin.

She rolled over revealing her exquisite ass and long slender legs. Once she settled, I began my leisurely assault on her lower half.

I found the little bottle and teased some oil into my hands then started again moving down along her strong back, the curve of her hips, the swell of her ass. I worked my way down agonisingly slow, deliberately digging my fingers into her muscles, drawing from her all the sounds of hunger and desire for more—more touch, more pleasure, more torturous delight.

I worked up her right foot, moving slowly to her calf then the thigh. She purred and winced at my careful lengthy strokes, deliberately provocative along her skin. I switched over to the other leg. My fingers traced her inner thighs, sliding up and down towards her heated pussy but never touching her, leaving behind a trace of what could have been. Empty, heated promises. She squirmed beneath me trying to push herself against my fingers. I chuckled at her failed attempts and moved on.

When I got to her ass, I had to stop myself from breaking it, slapping it, sinking my teeth into it like a ripe fruit; beautiful and bold, it teased me.

It was only fair I do the same.

I grabbed the bottle of oil and dripped it over her ass, watching the drops coat her skin and spill around her, across her, and into her. My cock twitched with dark intentions as my palms crested the shape of her ass, folding and pulling, pushing and kneading.

My fingers, slick and slippery with the oil, slipped slowly to the opening of her ass. She gasped as I held it there.

"Do you trust me Mia?"

"Yes," she whimpered.

"Are you relaxed?" I breathed through gritted teeth.

"So relaxed." She said, even as she squeezed her small, tight asshole.

I smirked, and pulled my hand away.

"You know, I hear these things can have happy endings."

"You've *heard*?" Her words were muffled from beneath the table.

"I want you to trust me Mia."

She pulled out her head and turned to me. "I do," she smiled at me and I unbuckled my belt. Her eyes followed my every move.

"Good." I approached the table and locked eyes with her, "Bring your wrists together and push them through the head hole."

Her eyebrows came together in question.

She paused.

I waited.

I swallowed my doubt.

Breath held, belt in hand.

My knuckles tightened against the leather.

After what seemed like a lifetime, she shifted backwards and put her wrists together and slid them into the head hole.

I grabbed her wrists and looped my belt around them attaching her to one of the legs.

"This is really uncomfortable Gabriel." She twisted her hands trying to find a comfortable perch—just what I had hoped.

I stood at the side of the table still looking into her eyes—looking for doubt or fear, and I found none. "You will have a better angle if you shift forward, tuck your knees in and get your ass in the air."

She paused, as if allowing my words to sink in. Slowly, Mia followed my instructions, allowing me to guide her body.

"How does that feel?"

"Better," she exhaled a shaky breath, "exposed."

"Beautiful." I took a leisurely trip around the table, allowing myself to appreciate her beauty; her perfectly rounded back, her sweet, lovely ass, and the curly, black hair that decorated the edge of her glistening lips. She was mesmerising. She was bound and she trusted me implicitly. My chest expanded with joy, my pants expanded with need.

I unbuttoned my shirt deliberately slow, watching Mia. She hovered somewhere between desire and uncertainty. I let my shirt drop to the floor as her hands tugged against my belt and her body swayed a little, unease settling in. I unbuttoned my pants and pulled them off watching her plump lips glisten as she bit and nibbled at them.

I threw my boxers aside and edged to the back of the table. Mia shivered as I traced the line of her body with a single finger. I hopped on the table, settling on my knees behind her. I grabbed the bottle of oil and squeezed it, letting the oil drip across her back. The drops spread like snakes, slithering into her hair and along her shoulders, down towards her breasts and into the splendid parting of her ass.

She gasped as I tucked my erection between her ass cheeks and leaned over her, caging her with my body and folding over her.

I allowed my hands to wander, to be guided by the slippery oil. I gilded over her slicked, naked skin, my chest slipped against her back as my hands flowed like a river around her body, the oil allowing my movements to run all over her unhindered.

I spread the oil with my palms, my chest, my cock, tracing the beautiful landscape of her body. My fingers tangled in her flesh, sinking into her flawless skin, flooding her senses. I spread the oil across every inch of her, of me. The oil made us one, moulding into one another like moving artwork, allowing me to slither against her.

She gasped and crooned at my touches. She was saturated with desire, flushed with need, fighting her restraints, wanting more, wanting me—I could tell in the desperate movements of her body, the way she pushed herself against me—wanting me inside her.

I moved back a fraction and she moaned her displeasure, throwing her head back, and my entire body stiffened.

My hands grabbed her hips, squaring them in front of me. I slid my fingers down to her wetness and she moaned against me, my hands froze as I brought my finger to the opening of her ass. She stilled. I could feel the squeeze as the tip of my finger touched the delicate, unbroken skin.

"Tell me not to Mia." I rasped at her, anticipation coating my skin like the oil. She panted and remained silent

My other hand slipped to her wet pussy and began to circle in slow deliberate movements. She moaned and, with the delectable sound of her pleasure, the tip of my finger slipped into her ass. She sucked in a sharp breath at the intrusion.

"Relax Mia." I used my right hand to stroke her swollen clit as the finger of my left hand slipped deeper into her ass, tight and frightened.

She gasped as my finger sunk in all the way. "Do you like that Mia?"

"Mm Mm." She tried. Her hips already grinding against my hand.

I stilled my hands and she whimpered in protest trying to push against me, into me. I remained frozen, "Do you want a happy ending?"

"I do." She begged with a rasping breath.

I did too.

My hand circled and rubbed her as she grated against me in desperation. It was beautiful and cruel watching her work so hard for her pleasure. My cock twitched and ached waiting to be inside her. Torture had two sides, two victims, but I knew this was the kind of pain we both wanted to endure; the pain that ended in exquisite unparalleled pleasure.

My finger sank in and out of her ass as she ground herself against my fingers, bringing herself closer to the edge—shaking, writhing, and thrashing until with a violent cry she smashed against me, breaking out in spasmodic vibrations, ecstasy dripping from her flushed and hungry body.

I pulled my fingers away then plunged my cock into her warm wet pussy, riding the waves of her ecstasy, allowing her to squeeze around me, pulling me in deeper, desperate, and harder until I too fell over the edge.

When I caught my breath, I slipped off her and stood by the table, watching as her body fell back to earth.

"Are you okay beautiful Mia?"

"Yes," she whispered, giving me a radiant smile, "Can you untie me?" She pulled against the belt as if I had forgotten it was there.

"I could but I love seeing you like this, exposed, vulnerable, and utterly fucking devastating." I captured her mouth in a kiss before she could protest then undid the belt buckle, setting her free.

I grabbed the towel and covered her ass, leaving her back exposed, "Lie down and finish your massage, I'll shower and pack."

"Pack?"

"Yeah, we're going away tonight?"

"We are? Where?" Her curiosity ignited delight behind her eyes.

"It's a surprise."

She opened her mouth to ask more questions, but I was already making my way to the foyer to get the masseuse back.

Maybe it was because I knew she was about to climb on my bike for the first time, but seeing her walk towards me in her tight jeans and new black leather jacket lit desire so fierce that I had to dig my nails into my palms to ground myself.

Her glistening lips shone red in the evening light as she approached, her mouth breaking into an appetising smile. I handed her the new helmet, she tucked it under her arm and laced her hand into mine as I led her to the Harley.

I climbed onto the bike and waited for Mia to climb up behind me, her body moulding into mine as she wrapped her arms around me. The sensation foreign and pleasant a smile rippled across my face.

"Ready?"

She nodded and answered with a muffled yes.

I started the engine, enjoying the vibrations that sang inside me. I could feel Mia's body coil tighter around me as I put the bike into gear and opened up the throttle. The bike jerked forward and we tore down the road. The world flew by us just outside our periphery. On the bike, we were in our own universe, listening to the white noise around us, as it fell under the roar of the engine and swung in the wind, turning into music. We bathed in the vulnerably, the exposure to the elements and the traffic. We were immune to the dullness of those cooped up in their four wheeled boxes, breathing stale air. We were exhilarated, traveling at rapturous speeds. Everything else simply fell away as I pushed the Harley to its limits, and we were flying three feet above the ground.

Every now and then Mia's hold would get tighter and she squeezed herself closer, gluing her body to my own, setting me alight. Blood hammered in my veins as my heart sung in an unfamiliar tune.

The city fell away and the road was all that lay ahead. We rode and, for a split second, I felt that everything was going to be okay.

I turned into a side road, it was narrower and isolated and the engine seemed so much louder in the falling darkness. I followed the snaking road, arched by a canopy of trees their limbs folded above our heads, reaching for one another as if desperate to touch. I understood their need. The archway dimmed the light, sealing us in a long darkening tunnel. The thought made me quiver, and I opened the throttle emerging on the other side in front of a classical farmhouse.

The farmhouse was European in nature, maintaining all the sentimental qualities one comes to expect in a farmhouse of this size. The wooden cladding around the house painted white and glowing orange against the setting sun. A long porch surrounded the house and dormer windows in perfect symmetry gave the building a nostalgic feeling.

I stopped but did not turn off the engine. In the silence, the purr travelled further filling the very air with its intensity. I pulled off my helmet and we waited. Behind me, Mia fidgeted and looked around. I could feel her curiosity peak as her body moved and turned behind me, her helmet bumping into the back of my head when she flung her head from side to side taking it all in. I could feel her growing tension, she wanted to know more. I smiled relishing in her reaction, her desires.

The front door opened and light spilt across the porch. A man walked out and approached us. He wore a worn pair of jeans and a T-shirt despite the chill in the air, and a large toe peaked out from one of his socked feet.

"Hello," he smiled from beneath a thick moustache that crawled along his lip like a fat caterpillar, "You must be Gabriel."

"Yes. Geoffrey?"

"Geoff is fine." He extended his arm and we shook briefly. "Welcome," he reached into the pockets of his jeans and produced a small bunch of keys and handed them over to me, "Just keep following the path and down to your left."

"Thank you."

"If you need anything, just call up to the main house." His moustache wiggled as his smile stretched.

"Thank you." I drove off, leaving the man standing in our wake.

The ride was short and almost leisurely. The breeze whipped my face, pushing the smell of manure and damp earth into my nose making my eyes tear.

I pulled up to a small unit. It seemed like a miniature copy of the larger house, having all the classic symmetry and twice the charm.

I switched off the engine and the world fell silent.

We climbed off the bike, and Mia pulled her helmet off eyeing the structure and spinning around taking in our surroundings. Her gaze shifted over to me.

"What are we doing here Gabriel?"

"Do you like it?"

"It's beautiful here," she looked up, a dusting of stars already scattered across the darkening sky. "So peaceful."

I smiled and unlocked the door, holding it open for Mia as she stepped inside.

We were greeted by a small foyer where we dropped our helmets and slipped out of our shoes. The room opened up to a small sitting area with a single couch set in front of a fireplace which was already lit and colouring the interior a warm amber.

To the left was a kitchenette with a dining room table tucked against one wall, and to the right a single bed made up with dark sheets.

I stepped inside and dropped our backpack on the bed while Mia hurried to the fireplace warming her back and hands at the roaring flames.

"Do you like it?"

"I just love it," she beamed with delight and my heart squeezed, joy leaking into my insides.

"Good. I wanted to do something special for your birthday."

Mia's cheeks flushed and she flashed me a row of white teeth, "I thought you already did that." Her cheeks turned a deep crimson and she bit her lip, making my body tighten with the memory. Her eyes roamed the room, focusing on anything but me. "It is beautiful though, thank you. But dinner would have been enough."

"Are you hungry?" I eyed her.

Mia bit her lower lip, "Ravenous."

"Me too." I growled.

She squealed when I lunged at her as she rounded the couch. I kept stalking her, and Mia giggled and danced and ran and shrieked as we played her game. She stepped to the right and I double stepped catching her, pinning her to the wall capturing her mouth in mine, crushing her body against my own.

The kiss was wild and hungry and left me wanting as I wrenched myself away and licked my lips, "Perhaps I'll have you for dessert."

Mia shivered at my words.

I entered the kitchen leaving Mia breathless and breath-taking against the wall.

She bit her lower lip and followed me, sitting onto the arm of the couch, "What are you doing?'

"Making you dinner."

"He cooks?"

"He does." I smirked.

"So many talents." She threw at me.

I shrugged, "This is the first time I have ever cooked for anyone but myself, so I've never had my food judged before." My core coiled with the gravity of my statement.

"Mmmm." She played, pretending I said nothing at all, "Well then I'll await my five star meal."

"If that's what you're after, you'll be waiting a very long time."

She guffawed at my remark, "But I'm hungry." She whined.

"I guess I'll just have to do."

Her eyes travelled along my face, down my torso and all the way down to my feet then back up again. Her face flushed and my heart thumped, "Guess you will." Her mouth broke into a sweet smile and my core twisted and knotted.

I sucked in a long breath and concentrated on what I was doing. Mia was distracting me, and I had work to do.

It was never about the food. It was about making something for someone other than myself; it somehow felt big and important. I was sharing of myself, carving out chunks of my being and handing it to another human to partake. It was magnificent and scary as hell.

The bacon was crispy and the eggs were over easy. I lightly toasted the bread and chopped a few slices of tomato. I grabbed the bottle of wine from the fridge and poured her a glass, grabbing myself a beer. I placed our dinner on the dining room table and sat across from her.

I stared at her as she spread the egg yolk across her bread like butter then placed bacon on the slice and bit into the open sandwich. The toast crunched in her mouth and she purred and nodded as she chewed.

I raised an eyebrow waiting, my heart chugging in my chest.

"Jury is out." She mocked, a sly grin spread across her lips.

I raised my beer, "Happy birthday Mia." She clinked her glass against mine, and I took a long sip.

"I know it's not much…" I started, but her hand landed on my own.

"Don't. I love it," she squeezed my hand, "You can ride a bike, fix broken things and cook. You'll make an excellent husband one day."

I coughed, choking on my beer, "Husband?" I cleared my throat.

"And father."

She had a look in her eye, something I'd never met before. She wanted more, she wanted a future. It scared me.

"I don't want to be a father." I grabbed my beer trying to drown out the sensation that was slowly climbing up my throat.

"Why?"

"I don't want to talk about it."

The fire crackled around us as a heaviness settled with the silence.

Mia cleared her throat and tried again, "So how did you learn to cook so well? I mean you have all these world class chefs at your beck and call..."

"I wasn't always as fortunate as I am now." I winked at her and hoped she wouldn't pry further. She knew my history, she knew about Alice and long days with an empty stomach. I wanted to celebrate, make her feel special and not rehash my past.

Talking to Mia often felt like walking a tightrope. Too many subjects were off limits—too much history, too much pain— neither of us wanted to think about. If we pushed or pulled too hard, one of us would wobble, feel off balance.

Neither of us was ready to fall.

We ate the rest of our meal in silence. Mia cleaned her plate with the last of her toast and sipped the rest of her wine, "That was delicious, thank you." I topped up her drink and got up, clearing the table.

"He cleans up after himself too."

The cutlery clunked as it crashed into the sink, "If you'd been paying attention while you stayed at the garage with me, you would have noticed it was always clean."

She shrugged and sipped her wine, "I was too busy looking at other things." She didn't try to hide the huskiness of her voice as her eyes took a leisurely journey down and back up my body.

I smirked at the compliment and grabbed another beer. "You're not so bad yourself," I tipped my chin forwards and cocked an eyebrow. Stalking to the couch where she sat, her cheeks flushed as I slid next to her and looked into her eyes, "Some might say perfect."

I sipped on my beer as she digested the word.

"You shouldn't say that."

"I can say whatever I want about you."

"Stop putting me on a pedestal of perfection, you don't know anything about me Gabriel."

I locked eyes with her, "What I do know, is that over the last ten years I've developed a very particular taste. With Alice, I didn't get to have anything, but now, with the amount of money I have, I have acquired a more particular taste. I only get the *very* best of everything. I don't settle for second best, only the most precious, the most expensive, the most *perfect*." I stretched out the word like elastic in my mouth, the T falling off the tip of my tongue with an iron clad certainty.

"Stops saying shit like that."

"Why?"

"Cause I don't like it."

"Not good enough."

"Drop it Gabriel."

"Why?!" I demanded my voice harsher than I meant.

"Because," she looked at the red liquid in her glass, "When you say shit like that it makes me feel vulnerable, like you actually mean it." She sipped on her wine and grabbed the bottle topping up her drained glass.

"What's wrong with that?"

"I am scared." She looked at me, her jaw clenched.

"Why are you scared Mia?"

She took a long sip and sighed, "Because I love you, you asshole," her eyes shot to mine and the entire world stopped for a singular magnificent second.

"You better say that again slowly." I growled.

"You're an asshole." Her mouth stretched in a sly grin.

"Mia!"

"I love you."

I sat, allowing her words to colour the grey of my life, to fill in the empty black corners with light and chase the cold away. I didn't answer; not because I didn't know to my core that I felt the very same, but because words are cheap and get thrown around like beads at Mardi Gras.

I have never been a man of many words but always of action, and I was going to show her with everything I had just how I felt; because actions scream so much louder than words, and my Mia would scream my name over and over until I finished with her.

"Say it again." I purred at her as I slid closer, my mouth grazing the delicate skin of her ear.

"I love you." She exhaled the words and I inhaled them, sucked them from her lips as my mouth smashed around hers.

"Luce mia." I groaned as I tasted her sweetness, the fruity flavour of her wine ripe on her tongue. She was a goblet full to the brim with liquor and sweet things, and I was about to drink from her, indulge in her gifts until I consumed all of her.

I took Mia's hand and pulled her from the couch. "Stand up Mia," my voice was scratched and gruff, she stood up to her full length and I loomed over her, taking her in, sucking in her perfume and boring into her eyes the golden flakes jumping in anticipation.

I stroked the line of her chin, slowly tracing it with a light touch, bringing my thumb to her lips and sweeping them slightly with the most tender of touches. She purred at my touch. My hands reached for her jeans, undid the button and tugged. "You won't need these," I whispered into her ear. Mia pulled them off leaving them in a puddle on the floor.

I pressed my body forwards, forcing hers onto the arm of the couch. "Sit Mia," I growled at her and she obeyed.

I traced the line of her jaw and brought my fingers to her chin, ensuring she looked into my eyes. I wanted to see her, into her, watch as I touched her, felt her, devoured her; she was mine and I was going to make certain she knew.

Not breaking eye contact, I reached for her shirt and

begun to unbutton it one button at a time, revealing a lacy black bra holding a pair of perfectly perky breasts. She gasped as I pushed the left one out of its cup and reached for her nipple already hardening. I pinched it lightly, and Mia's chest rose and her eyes fell away.

"Eyes on me!"

Mia's eyes locked on mine and I rewarded her with a delicate kiss, sucking her nipple into my mouth and tugging it with my teeth. I watched the need spill into her eyes and my body tightened with its own desires.

My hand reached over to her other breast and, like the first, I pulled down the cup. Her exposed breasts were held up neatly allowing me to pinch and roll her nipples—taste, tease, tug.

Mia's thighs rose, her legs began to shake, her breaths became shallow.

"Stop moving," my voice brought us both to a halt, "Eyes on me." I reminded her as I took a step back admiring my handy work. Her beautiful nipples stood to attention, the pink, plump tips hardened and glistening against the fire light.

Her lips parted and eyes dilated, her breath hitched—she looked fucking delectable. The fire crackled painting her body honey and ochre, and all I wanted was to lick it all from her body—all the sweetness and goodness—and make it all mine, letting it saturate my insides so that I too could become good and sweet. Except I had dark desires that I was about to impart and I hoped her goodness could withstand my ruthlessness.

I walked back to the couch and put my hands on her knees, "Open!"

Mia parted her thighs willingly. My fingers traced the lines of her outer thigh and rounded her ass, grabbing the elastic of her silky, black panties and pulled them off revealing her beautiful, pink pussy. Instinctively she closed her legs.

"I said open! Don't let them close again or there will be consequences, do you understand?"

"Yes Gabriel," her voice was shallow and deep. My name on her lips sent a shiver around my body that ricocheted against my heart.

I forced her knees further apart, and she found purchase on the couch, arching her back and throwing her head back.

"You are incredible," My voice grated against her skin as I fell to my knees, kissing the silken length of her thigh, her scent rising to torment my senses and tamper with my sanity. My nails dug into her flesh, and she cried out as my tongue tasted her. She was heat and honey, and I savoured her flavour as my tongue flicked and lashed against her wet lips. Relishing a long, slow ride of delight that drew desperate moans from Mia and made me more rigid, engorged, and hungry. I devoured her in a tender assault of the senses. Her hands clutched fistfuls of my hair, pulling me against her, her hips moving against my mouth—wanting more, wanting me, wanting control.

I pulled away from her and she whimpered, her need searing and raw.

"Not yet luce mia," I whispered against her and bit the swollen soft flesh of her breast. She cried out and the sound ignited the maddening wildness that brewed beneath our gentleness.

I ripped her from the couch and pushed her to her knees. Her shaking hands reached for my jeans, tearing at the zipper, scratching at the button as she pulled them down freeing me. Her hands circled along my shaft and she pulled me into her hot mouth, ripping a primal, guttural growl from me.

I sank my fingers into her hair and yanked her up. My

cock pulled from her mouth with a pop, and we both groaned our disappointments.

I spun Mia around and bent her over the arm of the couch, forcing her legs apart with my own and pressing her head below the arm of the couch where it locked.

"I don't want you to move Mia."

She whimpered her response, her chest rising and falling as I prowled around her fighting the onslaught of raw physical desire and my need to possess her. If I was going to show her how much I loved her, I had to show her what love really was—a long torturous path, full of anguish and pain that ends in fantastic pleasure. My need to make her suffer with need defied reason, but I didn't care. I was possessed by her —infected with Mia.

I positioned myself behind her, my hard cock between her wet lips, and I moved ever so slowly. My cock slid against her as my hands explored her skin with feather light touches. She shivered beneath me, her moans growing with each movement, her legs quivering. She wanted to move against me but she was trapped, her head pushing against the unmoving couch. She was a prisoner and torturing her was insanely satisfying.

I kept sliding against her and the more she tried to push against me—trying to force my body to please hers—the slower my movements became.

"Please Gabriel." She begged as her whimpers became mewls of desperation, her legs shaking with need, her face an anguished mask of agony.

I was stripping her sanity bit by bit, pushing her to her limits, and pushing myself over a cliff I have always wanted to fall down. It was a kind torment; a delectable agony, a wild and fierce possession of all her senses, a disillusion of mine. It was purity and beauty in its rarest form. We were a broken fucked up diamond, and I was about to carve us to a million dazzling pieces.

"Tell me Mia, say the words."

"Gabriel…"

"Say them."

"I.Love.You." Her ragged breath fell from her as the words tumbled in a strained, shaky voice, and my heart seized as they sneaked inside—settling, spreading, and infecting my soul.

I tumbled into the abyss and slammed into her; she cried in pleasure, in pain, in despair and in relief. I withdrew, slower this time and slid home again. Home. She was my home. I grabbed her hips, my fingers digging into her clammy body saturated in sweat and sex like a fever. Maybe I infected her too.

My cock drove into her, fuelling the frenzied madness that brewed between us; a demented, throbbing need that spiralled into untamed urgency that neither of us had any control over. It raged through us like a scorching deluge, shredding our sanity and stripping us raw to our need. I smothered her with my body, answering the desperate way she pushed into my thrusts. My body grew rigid, my grip tighter—bruising—as Mia splintered around me and we fell.

We tore apart seeking comfort in each other's arms, seeking to regain a perch in this world, a semblance of sanity.

We fell back and I pulled us away from the couch and onto the cold bed, breathless and senseless.

I held her as if she was the only real thing in this world, an anchor. Mia pulled me to her, clawing her way back to me.

"Mia, luce mia." I managed.

"Gabriel…" she tucked herself into me, curling against my heated skin—wasted, exhausted, and elated. She closed her eyes and we both melted into the darkness.

orning light pierced through drawn curtains in a fine, sharp line. Like a splinter, my entire world shattered in the most beautiful and petrifying ways. My heart swelled and chugged as I thought of Mia calling my name, and my skin crawled with warmth as she uttered the words, "I love you Gabriel."

I pulled her body to me and relished in her warmth, her scent, and her beauty. She mumbled into her pillow and I chuckled. Mia was not a morning person.

"Why are you up already?"

"It's already late and we still have one more thing to do before we head back."

She mumbled something incoherent and tried to pull away from me. I pulled her closer to me and held on to her.

"I thought you said we had to get up."

"I am up." I bit her shoulder as I ground my hardness against her ass.

"You are insatiable Gabriel."

"Can you blame me?"

"Let me go. I stink."

"You smell incredible," and she did—of me and sex and jasmine. I nibbled her ear.

"I'm gross."

"You're stunning." I kissed the curve of her shoulder.

"Let me go." She whined, and I grinned against her long neck.

"Beg me."

She huffed and I tightened my grip around her, my erection sliding between her legs.

"Beg Mia."

"Gabriel," she whined again as my cock slid against her wetness, shadows of the night before echoing between us.

"Beg." I hissed as I nibbled her neck, my teeth sinking into her flesh.

"Please Gabriel."

"What are you begging for Mia?"

"Gabriel…"

"Do you want me to let you go?"

"Never let me go Gabriel." Her voice trembled.

I purred at the words, "Now say it"

I loosened my grip but didn't release her fully.

"Say.It." I gritted my teeth.

"Gabriel…" she whispered as my arms hardened around her in a threat to cage her in again, my erection still sliding along her wetness.

"I love you."

"Mm mm. I fucking love when you say that." I rolled above her and captured her mouth in mine. I didn't care about the frizzy morning hair or tired eyes, I just wanted to show her each and every fucking moment that I felt the same.

My swelling erection slid against her wetness—grinding, teasing, wanting.

"Gabriel…" she moaned into my mouth, and I felt myself harden even more.

I slipped inside her, a deep growl emanating from somewhere inside me, something primal and needy that felt her and demanded her everywhere.

I kissed her as I moved inside her; I wanted my lips and my tongue to say all the words that hung on their edge but that I was unable to say. I wanted to create our own language —a language only our bodies understood, a language that our heat and need translated to desire and desperation that was bigger than ourselves.

Her nails bit into my skin as she stole my breath with her burning moans. I dragged my mouth from hers just so I can watch her face as it grimaced and tore into joy and delight, as her full lips pulled and pouted, breathlessly beckoning me as her eyes fluttered shut. Her fevered skin coloured and her body quivered as she fell in final surrender. My flesh fused in hers, my need urgent and desperate as she pulled me apart and consumed all that was left of me.

"Luce mia." I uttered the words against her searing flesh. I found her mouth and kissed her greedily falling on my back and releasing her at last.

"Are you going to do that every time I say I love you?"

"Why don't you say it again and find out?"

She bit her lip, a smile spreading across her glowing face, "You're incorrigible Gabriel."

"I can't help what your words do to me, Mia."

Our eyes locked for a second and I saw a flicker of something in hers. It was momentary and fleeting, and she tore her eyes away from mine and got off the bed.

I watched her walk into the bathroom and moments later the taps came on. I reached for the phone by the bedside and called the main house.

"Hello." A male voice answered after the third ring.

"We're ready."

"Excellent. We will be down in thirty minutes."

I hung up and made my way to the shower, hoping Mia would tell me again that she loved me.

"Why do you keep looking at your watch?" She looked stunning with her makeup-free face and wild, wet hair that hung around her like loose ropes.

The knock on the door was my response.

"Let's go."

I shot up and opened the door. Geoff stood outside, his thick moustache stretching across his face. He wore a large hat that covered his hair and sunglasses that were too big for his face.

"Good morning, I trust you had a good night?"

I nodded while Mia's face flushed in crimson.

"Should we get going?"

I grabbed Mia's hand and stepped outside as we followed the farmer to a golf cart that waited at the end of the lane. We hopped on and took off. In the morning light, the farm seemed to stretch on for miles. Green pastures surrounded the lush, green property as the buggy turned lazily around paved paths.

The smell permeated the air, it changed and soured around us from fresh earth to pungent, old sweat. Mia stiffened next to me and we rounded a sloping corner. The large shed was as manicured as the house and the lawns, made of oak planks and a sloping corrugated iron roof that was painted a too-bright-red.

Geoffrey parked the buggy and stepped out leading us towards the stables. We bypassed the building, walking around it to a fenced oval pasture. Mia grew rigid as a second man came into view.

He rode a white horse that seemed to be wearing long black socks, while leading two others in his wake—one Chestnut, the other bay coloured. The horses were in full riding gear, galloping along the fence.

Geoffrey put two fingers to his mouth and blew out a short, sharp whistle. The man whipped his head around and when he saw us, kicked the stirrups and lead the horses towards us.

I could feel Mia's body harden as the beasts approached us. I put it to excitement as my own heart constricted with joy.

I've never been to a working farm before; well, not in the sunlight and not one where I didn't burn everything down, and I've never ridden a horse. The lead horse snorted and shook his head as the three neared us and I resisted the urge to take a step back. I've never backed away from anything, I wasn't about to now.

Geoffrey climbed the fence, his hands hanging over the white wood. He reached for the horses as they approached allowing them to smell his hand and he patted the one nearest to him along the cheek, burying his face against the long snout. When he turned to us his face beamed.

"This here is Garnet and she's a beauty. Max will ride her as he guides you today, and these here are BONNIE & CLYDE." I eyed Geoffrey and he burst out laughing.

"Don't worry, they're not outlaws." His laughter boomed out of him like thunder rolling across the green field.

"So why the names?"

"They were just inseparable," his glance pivoted from my face to Mia and back again, "We bought them from another farmer who said he couldn't break either one in. I found that hard to believe, I've never owned a horse that didn't work for a livin'." He patted Garnet's long, white neck and they shared a long look, the horse's long white lashes hooded its eyes. "Once we got 'em over here, we placed them in their stalls, one on each end of the stable. They went mad, kicking and snorting, until we put them side by side. I'll be honest, I've never seen two horses like them. Once we started training them, we found that they wouldn't break alone. They resisted, they retaliated, but as soon as we put them together it was like a calm settled over them," he reached over to Clyde and patted the long neck, "I think this old rascal just needed a girl to show him what's what." He chuckled and the horse shook his head.

"My wife suggested we call them Romeo and Juliet, but their story was far too tragic."

I frowned at his words, "As was Bonnie and Clyde's."

He rubbed his chin considering my words and shrugged, "Perhaps, but at least they went down like they lived—wild and well and together." A strange smile crossed his face and he patted Clyde once more, "Don't worry, as long as they stay together everything will be fine."

But if they didn't stay together? I wondered as he turned to Max and gave him instructions. I wrapped my arm around Mia and pulled her close, she felt distant and was yet to utter a word since we arrived.

"Are you ok? I thought you would be a little more excited," I turned to look at her face and noticed her eyes, tears pooled at the rims, "Mia?"

"No," she reached for me and placed a hand on my chest, "There's just…" here eyes swung from her hands to the horses and back to me, "Gabriel, I—"

"We don't have to ride if you're not ready."

"No, that's not it."

"Mia?"

"It's—"

"Would you like to feed the horses?" Geoffrey interrupted as he approached us with a bucket full of hay and some chopped up vegetables. He paused and stammered when he saw Mia.

She wiped her eyes with the back of her hand and plastered a fake ass smile on her face. I'm not sure who she thought she was fooling, "Yes, let's feed the horses."

She stepped towards Geoffrey and accepted a handful of veg from him. I followed suit wondering if I pushed too soon, maybe she wasn't ready for horses or for reminders.

I grabbed a handful of hay and vegetables and mimicked Mia. She hung over the fence, her hand outstretched to Bonnie. I held mine over towards Clyde who took a few steps towards me. The massive horse sniffed then began chewing.

Geoffrey grabbed my wrist, "Open your hand with a straight palm, friend."

I looked to Mia who opened her cupped hand too. She must've been overwhelmed being so close to horses again, horses that resembled her Cookie and Jigsaw so perfectly. I berated myself again but was drawn back to Clyde who was frothing at the mouth just lightly, the bit tucked into his mouth pulling against the lips. He chewed the food from my hand leaving a slimy layer of saliva, which I wiped all over the back of my jeans.

"Right. Now that the introductions are all done, you best be on your way before these two get restless. Max here has warmed them up, and they're ready to go."

He handed us each a helmet and indicated that there would be no more talking until we both wore them. The clip clicked into place and I turned back to Clyde.

I looked at the horse, studying the creature from beyond the barrier of the fence and questioned my sanity as Geoffrey's voice cut through my doubts.

"Climb over the fence and stand on the second rung than grab a hold of the horn, that's that rounded looking handle at the front of the saddle. When you feel balanced, swing your foot over, get yourself into the saddle, and your feet in the stirrups. I'll double check your length once you're on."

I glanced from Geoffrey to Clyde and back again. Geoffrey was already halfway over the fence, "Don't worry, I'll even hold him for you."

I wasn't really worried. Not *really*.

I climbed over the fence and grabbed onto the horn, it was solid and comforting as I swung my weight over from the fence to the horse. Clyde shuffled a little as I adjusted myself in the saddle.

"Now, grab the reins till Max takes over." I did as I was told, feeling the horse's powerful muscles ripple beneath me as he flicked his head from side to side, his mane whipping before me. Geoffrey adjusted my stirrups and patted Clyde along the neck, whispering something to the horse. Sitting in the saddle, I touched the animal's neck, patting and stroking it like Geoffrey had. Clyde twitched his ears and took a few steps back. He smelt of the earth—a dark, rooty fragrance with flinty undertones. It made me feel safer, and for a second I wondered how my smell made him feel.

My body tightened and I gripped the reins as Geoffrey spun me around then let go of the horse, leaving me floating on the back of the beast.

"Do you need help there, miss? Gabriel there said you used to ride, so I just assumed…"

"I'm fine." She was panting, her body leaning forward and her knuckles white on the horn as she adjusted herself on the saddle.

"You sure?" Geoffrey tightened her stirrups.

"I said I was fine." She was more firm that time.

Geoffrey shrugged and produced a sound like one of his horses, "Best grab the reins then, miss."

I studied Mia, my brow cocked, and uncertainty fell inside me like the first winter snow. It settled in the pit of my stomach; Mia wasn't ready.

Before I had time to finish the thought Max was beside me clicking his tongue and Clyde took off in a slow gentle walk around the paddock, walking along side Garnet. As we walked, Max gave me a crash course in horse riding.

It was already uncomfortable. I didn't see the attraction, but Mia loved horses enough to keep their pictures by her bedside table. It made her happy. These gentle giants made her happy. So, I would try to like it, to bare it, even if just for a day. Because, I realised I was willing to do anything that would make Mia happy. Looking back, I guess that's where I went wrong. But we'll get to that.

Geoffrey opened the gate and Max led us out and down towards a path that veered away from the farm and into open countryside.

The world seemed different from the back of the horse, hypnotic almost. The horse's ears bobbed slowly in front of me as I rocked back and forth in the saddle. The crisp morning air blanketed us and the sun fought to penetrate the cold. Clyde's hoofed steps crunched along the gravel track, and he blew huge clouds of steam from his nostrils as he powered on.

I had to admit it was beautiful, and for a fleeting moment I thought of Alice. Maybe it was the cold that kissed my face or the trees shedding the last of their leaves, or all the open untouched space. I thought of the park and shivering under a thin blanket that did nothing to shelter me from the cold. I dismissed the thought. Alice didn't belong here with me and Mia and these fucking horses. I sucked in a long, cold breath that seared my throat and cleared my head.

My thighs and ass burned by the time the horses climbed to the top of a solitary hill. We stopped near a tree, whose burning orange and brown canopy still hung on and cast a long shadow across the lush green grass.

Max hopped off his horse and relieved it of the picnic basket and rug it had been carrying. He unfurled the rug in a long-practiced movement then lay the basket in one corner. He looked to Mia and I, who were still mounted.

"I'll be back in an hour. I'll just go walk them off and give them some water." The tip of his lips twitched in a smirk, "Do you need a hand dismounting."

I glared at him and uncurled my frozen hand from the reins and grabbed the horn, swinging myself off the horse. Everything pulled and screamed at me. Max shrugged and approached Mia, taking Bonnie's reigns. He hopped back onto Garnet and within a minute had disappeared down the path.

I sat on the rug, stretching my legs and flexing my aching hands. Mia tucked herself beside me and I laced my fingers with hers.

"Are you okay?" She nodded silently. The girl that I was with this morning, all of a sudden a completely different person, "I'm sorry it was insensitive of me, I should've asked you first. I thought you would be ready and excited."

She turned to look at me, "Oh but I am, it's all just so overwhelming." She ran a hand over her thigh.

"Would you like something to eat?" Even before I opened the basket, I could smell the freshly baked bread, the aroma rushing out of the basket and evaporating into the breeze. I rummaged inside and unpacked the contents. I laid the bread, cheeses, and fresh produce on the rug. I grabbed the bottle of water and a long red flask of coffee. I unscrewed the lid hoping the aroma would snap Mia out of whatever trance she had sunk into.

Mia was staring out in silence watching the world around us, listening to the buzzing of the insects and the whispering of the wind in the leaves. She looked at me, solemn and serious, tucking a loose strand behind her ear.

"What is it?" I asked pulling myself closer around her.

"Tell me why you don't want kids." The question took me by surprise.

"Why does it matter?" My brow gathered in a severe line above my eyes.

"Don't change the subject."

"I wasn't." I flexed my fists at my sides.

"You're answering a question with a question. Just tell me."

I raked a hand through my hair and sucked in a deep breath, "I don't want kids because I don't want to be responsible for another person I might not be able to take care of." Her face softened and her features changed. A warmth radiated from her, one that screamed of compassion and empathy. I didn't want either.

"I don't want a piece of my heart walking outside of my body twenty-four hours a day without having any control of what's going to happen. It's too hard. I'm already responsible for you and Spots…"

"You can't control *everything* Gabriel."

"Exactly. Look at what happened to Simone—to you. Life

is fucking cruel," my heart stammered, "I don't want to bring a kid into the world and watch it suffer."

"So, don't watch it suffer."

I exhaled my frustration, "It's not that easy. I couldn't live with myself if anything happened..." I rubbed a hand over my face, "Anyway, any kid would deserve better. No one deserves a piece of shit dad like me."

"But you're not a piece of shit."

"You have no idea what I am," I stilled for a second, my heart smashing against my chest, "Why are you pushing this hard? Are you...?" I let the words fall to the ground like the autumn leaves, a cold spear of fear pierced my heart.

She just shook her head. The relief was immediate and she flashed me a sad look, "Tell me about them. Tell me about the kids Gabriel."

I put my bread down, my appetite suddenly gone. I've told her everything else, I guess it was time to come clean about what I did with Tony's legacy.

PART XX

The dead screamed at me from their void. Lost souls of victims that never got a chance. Their childhood taken away by the swipe of a pen or the point of a finger.

Once I took care of Judge Crabb, I knew I had lit a match and the explosion that would follow would be devastating.

So I hid—buried in dog shit and love. Simone afforded me the shelter I needed without knowing it. For a brief while, I might have even believed that everything happened for a reason. Spots got hurt so that I could be saved; but then I looked at his mangled leg and wet eyes, and I knew there was no meaning or reason, only me.

Whatever I touched turned to shit.

During the days when I lived at the dog rescue, I would help Simone. I cleaned and washed dogs, fed them, learning how to interact with the friendly ones and how to avoid the aggressive ones. I learned that patience and calmness often turned their attitudes. Simone provided them with love, enough from the both of us I guess; so when they warmed to her, they also accepted me like I was an inseparable part of her, like her shadow.—not really there, not really real. Or maybe it was the darkness they sensed inside me.

I allowed their affection and slobber to slide off me as I kept myself detached, saving the empathy I had left for Spots.

Dogs are akin to people, and they taught me a few very valuable lessons. Just because they're friendly and let you pet them, doesn't mean they won't turn on you in a second and bite your hand off. Just because they let you approach, doesn't mean they want to be your friend. Just because they've been hurt once and lash out, doesn't mean they don't need your love.

Simone managed to pry me open. Maybe it was her need to be with another human after spending so much time with animals that don't talk back in the same language, or maybe it was my need to feel closeness. We talked. She was like the mother I never had and the friend I never knew I needed. She allowed me to be angry about Alice and sad about Spots without any judgement. She didn't pamper me or spoil me, instead she made sure I earned everything and worked for it. She made me *want* to work for it. She made me want to get up and help her, she made me care—about her and her stupid beautiful, broken dogs. She made me want more for myself. She gave me the most dangerous gift a person could give another. Hope.

We made memories—good ones, happy ones like in that picture of hers. Somedays I still think we could have been on that wall together in a collection of happy moments that we shared. But I wasn't one for pictures and maybe she had all the broken memories she cared to hold on to.

At night after Simone turned her lights off, I would stay awake and dig through my treasure of despair. I grabbed the photos first and organised them into numbers from first to last. Then I cross referenced them with the names in the blue book. After the first month I had a list, the names of all the motherfuckers who sold their children to Tony for protection.

I remembered the faces, each haunted pair of eyes, and

naked, tortured piece of exposed flesh. Every night I promised them retribution as I fell into a fitful sleep.

By the end of the second month, I had compiled a list of addresses and work places. I knew what they each did and why they paid Tony but, best of all, I knew where their tapes where.

I was getting impatient, I wanted to act. But I was learning that to get a dog to trust you, you needed to take time, you need to make them comfortable and allow them to get to know you, to sniff your hand, come closer a little each day until you became their master.

By the end of the third month, Spot's leg was looking better and Salvatore finally made contact.

He showed up late one night, alcohol and perfume trailing him like a tail.

He greeted Simone who didn't seem happy to see him.

He cocked his head at her in greeting and she looked at me, her sharp gaze full of annoyance.

"I'll let you boys talk." She took her leave without saying another word.

"Where the hell have you been?"

"Keeping low."

"In someone's pussy?"

His mouth cracked into a smile, "Low is low..."

"When I said we needed to hole up, that's not what I meant," I shook my head in disgust. When he said nothing else, I led him into my room and closed the door behind us.

I pulled out the blue book and the lists I've made, "I've been working."

"That's good."

"We need a plan."

He nodded and we sat down. I showed him my lists. The more I spoke, the darker his expression got and the more sombre. A dark coldness fell on the room as if his mood was a colour, murky and angry. Salvatore refused to touch the book; he never came near it, as if it contained a deadly virus. I've never seen him scared before, but that book played with his mind, plagued it, just as it did my own.

"So, what are we going to do about this?" He hissed the question.

"We're going to burn those motherfuckers down."

"So, you're crawled out of your hole?" Lupe asked, his face a mask of calm. I knew that beyond it lay turbulent waters, "I was so sorry to hear about your girlfriend."

I swallowed his insult and ignored his bait.

"I'm here for your truce."

"Oh?" He tucked his hands behind his head as he leaned back into the chair, his feet still on the desk. "Ran out of ideas? Money? Time?"

The men around the room laughed. I remained calm.

"You're about four months too late boy."

"Here is my offer," I inhaled, "I want you to leave town and leave me alone. I will keep ownership of the car wash and you will buy it off me for a generous profit and then sell Tony's garage to me. All our business dealings in this matter will be legitimate, all transactions legal," As I spoke Lupe's smile widened as if I was a crazed man, "In return, I will give you my word that I will not release your tapes and, in a show of good faith, I will give you one." At that his smile cracked and fell away like plaster from a moulding wall, "*And* I'll even let your people decide whose tape you get."

Lupe sat for a while and rearranged his features. The anger behind the eyes blazed as he strained to keep his face expressionless.

"Anything else?"

"Yes."

His nostrils flared and eyes widened at my impertinence, "I want you to tell your men to leave me and mine alone."

"And if we refuse?"

"I will release all your tapes, but not to the authorities. To your wives and lovers, to your daughters and sons, to your business partners and your enemies." My words drifted off and filled the room.

Lupe's face twisted in a grimace and his legs fell off the table, his back straightened and he held his head high, his eyes blazing into mine.

"I'll get back to you."

As I got up, a long languid smile crossed his face, "Tell me, how's your dog doing?"

I clenched my jaw and locked eyes with the man, "This is a limited time offer, you have till 5pm tonight to give me your answer. And trust me, I will *not* come after your friends and dogs—I will come after *everyone*."

I turned away and walked out of the office.

I didn't go back to Simone's, knowing Lupe was having me watched now that I had shown my face again. I had no intention of putting Simone or Spots in danger again. I didn't meet up with Salvatore. Instead, I waltzed into the car wash like I owned the place which, according to all relevant paper-work, I did. Everyone's jaws fell open as they saw me strolling through the car wash up the stairs and into my bedroom. Someone else was staying there. It pissed me off, but not enough to really care. It was never home anyway.

I packed up what was left of my clothes and went to the office. I kicked out the random who sat at my desk and waited for the phone to ring.

It took them three hours and twenty-three minutes to accept my offer. The tape they asked for belonged to a higher up that had a taste for the morbid and macabre, the contents of which still makes my stomach churn.

I called Desmond. He wasn't happy to hear from me. I

wasn't surprised. I wanted to know about his next shift so that I could come collect the tape. Once plans were laid in place, I drove out of the city and gave Lupe's men the slip. If they knew the location of the tapes, it would all be over before it ever started.

When I met Lupe the following morning, he looked dishevelled and out of sorts unlike his usual kempt appearance. I guess his employers weren't too happy with how events played out. It made me glow from the inside out. Watching him squirm gave me insurmountable amounts of joy.

He sat across from me at the car wash, not the same man that walked in four months before following Tony's death. Everything has slipped out of his slimy hands, and I have no doubt he anticipated a six-foot pit that was awaiting him when he returned home with the tape. I wanted to feel sorry for the man but, really, I felt nothing—just joy at his impending demise.

"Do you have the tape?"

I guess we were no longer exchanging pleasantries or wasting time. "First I want the garage."

Lupe nodded at one of the other men who opened up a suitcase and pulled out a wad of paperwork. The papers were meticulous, the white glaring around the dark room. All the I's were dotted and T's crossed. "I think you'll find the offer for the car wash more than generous." Lupe's voice was curt as if it stung him to talk.

I took my time, stretching out his torment. He shifted in his seat as I took a leisurely read of the contract. It didn't matter, not really. I knew there was too much at stake for them to fuck this up for me, but watching that fucker squirm was something I didn't want to bypass.

When I signed the paperwork, I handed it back to the man whose sausage fingers grabbed the paper as if it was china. He placed it back in the suitcase.

"The money?"

"Already in your bank account."

I knew it was but I wanted to hear him say it. I nodded and reached for my top drawer, took out the tape and handed it over to Lupe. He snatched it from my hand then held it like a burning coal, shifting it from one hand to the next as if they were catching fire—it was too hot a commodity. He stashed it into his jacket.

"The garage?"

"Is evacuated as you requested. You can move in immediately, and I suggest you do as you are now trespassing." He gave me a smarmy grin, and I scoffed at his last effort to display any power.

I stood, signalling the meeting was over. The relief was visible across the room as shoulders fell like a Mexican Wave from each man across the room.

"Pleasure doing business with you Lupe."

"Let us both hope that neither of us has the pleasure again."

"That's the only thing that's come out of your mouth that I agree with." His mouth dropped open as I walked by him and to the door. I might have been twenty years his junior, but in the last four months since Tony's death, I had aged and grew. I fucking helped murder two people, and I had just blackmailed one of the largest crime syndicates in the world to hand over the garage. I felt cocky and brash as hell, and I strode out of that office like a peacock in heat.

When I walked out of that car wash, I never looked back. I walked all the way to the garage, with each step feeling Tony's chains slip off my ankles in loud clangs. Like a freed man I sucked in the air, it all felt more crisp, smelt fresher as if I was breathing it for the very first time.

I smashed through the iron door and right to my room.

Mine.

Someone else had been living there but I didn't care,

because as of that day I owned the fucking place, and I was going to make it my home.

Salvatore came over a few hours later. We quietly shared a beer, celebrating in our comfortable silence and considering what the future held.

We had time to figure that out. That night, that beer, it tasted sweeter than anything I had ever drank and the silence was filled with all the possibilities of everything that was to come. It filled me too, with hope. Maybe I was naïve, or maybe I was too young, but that night I took my first step to freedom.

Or so I thought.

W hen you plan a scorched earth strategy, there are two considerations: timing and the element of surprise.

In order to achieve those, I needed to be patient.

And so, I was.

A number of crucial things happened in that time and some others that are far less important, so I will only fill you in on the essentials.

The first, and perhaps most important, was that I became known. Word travelled fast of my new acquisitions.

Not just Hill Street and the garage, but Tony's rumoured tapes were suddenly a very real reality, and suddenly I was on everyone's radar. See, Tony led by fear but that was never my intention. I didn't want to break the dogs—well not yet— I wanted to become their friend, gain their trust, and then destroy them.

Construction began on Hill Street a week after my acquiring the garage. Simultaneously, I began to tear down Tony's throne and accidentally built myself an empire. I'm not talking about a castle or a fort which, in many ways, Hill

Street became—a fortified palace where I would always be safe, a master of the keep hiding in the highest room in the tallest tower.

I had amassed an accidental and extremely loyal army, and all it took was telling them they owed me nothing and loyalty wasn't something I wanted to buy. It was a lie of course. I needed them to worship me, to be prepared to die for me, and they were because I set them free and told them there were no strings attached. Thing was, they were too busy looking for strings when they should have been looking for a noose.

It started as a trickle. Men would visit me at the office, making casual conversation, probing as to my plans. Really what they wanted to know were my plans for them. I told them about Hill Street and the grand ideas I had, and they all offered to help. Of course they did—keep your enemies closer and what not. I was their enemy, one with a weapon so dangerous I could destroy them all.

I gained their trust by hiring their companies. I allowed Hill Street to be built on their greed and corruption while I laundered Tony's money and shook their hands; while I got invited to their homes and sat at the dinner table with their now grown kids—with their hollow eyes and empty expressions. I spent months feeling sick to my stomach while I smiled in their faces, cultivating a relationship, building trust, baiting them like the feral dogs they were—a bowl of milk closer each day until they finally stepped inside.

The launch of Hill street was one of the largest events the city has seen in years. It was lavish, over the top, and exuberant in every way. Celebrities I didn't recognise shook my hand and smiled as if they mattered. Any and all my new *friends* arrived with their wives pumped full of plastic and chemicals so they can look prettier and perkier. If you ask me, it was a freak show, a parade of ugliness that came from needles and doctor offices.

I greeted them all and endured their whispered come ons and too log handshakes that came with a wink or a bite of a lip behind their husband's backs. I smiled politely and held back the sourness that rose in my throat.

The alcohol inundated their senses and the music lulled their tongues. If I was a man like Tony I would have walked away rich. Rich with information, rich with a hundred ways to blackmail and taint, rich with deviance. Instead, I gave them a space where soft flesh and hard alcohol made them feel safe, where a few perky nipples made their wallets and tongues loose. I allowed it; for a single night, I allowed them to feel safe, content, calm even. I allowed them to believe that all of Tony's secrets were buried with him and I was a new brand of leader, one that would turn a blind eye and allow their misadventures without a cost.

But see, that's where they were wrong. The minute their name was written in Tony's book they were already indebted to me, to their children, and I was about to collect.

A few hours into the party I retreated into the hidden corridor and took my elevator to the Penthouse. I had never wanted to stay there, but it was necessary—at least for a short while. Keeping up appearances and such like.

I could hear the music from below, it vibrated through the entire building like a shudder.

I gazed at the crowd below as they spilt into the street like vomit. Ants running to their anthill, following a king that was about to slaughter them all.

I sipped at my whisky. It was getting warmer, the ice melting, turning the taste, diluting the alcohol and my senses. I threw it into the sink and grabbed a fresh tumbler and a new bottle. It was a gift from one of the men downstairs, a faceless ghost in the crowd. I think he thought I would accept it as payment for a transgression or two. I didn't. I took the bottle and broke three of his fingers. The crunch was like ice against glass, a unique sound, pure and utterly satisfying.

He grovelled, I forgave, and I kept the fucking whiskey.

I hoped the liquid fire would burn through my veins long enough to help me get through my task. I checked my watch again, it was nearing midnight. Problem was, when the clock struck twelve no one would turn into a pumpkin, and I would still be waiting. Waiting for the last of them to go home, unprepared, drunk, and unsuspecting.

I sucked in a long, deep breath, steeling myself, adding oxygen to the fire burning inside me, flaring the flames, and topped the rest of the alcohol into my mouth.

I took the emergency stairs two floors down and went into room 523. The boys were already waiting, sitting like sentinels, watching and preparing.

I found Salvatore leaning against the window and looking down into the world we had created.

"Is everything ready?"

"Are you?" He looked to me, his eyes set and serious.

"Don't worry about me, I've been ready for this day for almost two years."

He nodded then tipped his head to the thinning crowd, "They have no idea what's coming."

"That's the idea," my lips stretched across my face in thin line and my brow gathered, "Guess I better head back down stairs. Be seen…"

He nodded.

"I'll see you soon."

"Yes, you will boss."

I didn't bother acknowledging, just turned my back on Salvatore and headed back downstairs to the party.

The car glided along the bare highway, the lights too bright in the silence. I stank of booze and cheap perfume, and my sleeve bore the mark of lipstick from unwanted affection from women who should have kept their hands and mouths to themselves.

I stared out of the window, my blank eyes staring past my reflection and into the future.

I had sent teams all over the city that night and across the country. The scorched earth policy would be executed quietly—quietly and brutally.

But I wanted to be there for as many displays of violence as I could, for each retribution I could get to. Not because I had a blood lust or death wish, but because I wanted to see their faces as they were served what they deserved.

I was Troy.

I had built a giant building and those fuckers flocked to it in peace, completely unaware. They were fed, their thirst was quenched by endless alcohol. I made sure each and every one of them felt totally at ease as they headed to their homes. What those assholes didn't know was what awaited them as they went to sleep that night.

Lucky for them, I was about to show them.

I picked Pete Monroe because I wanted to watch him suffer the most. I'll be honest, the man was more crooked than a banker's smile, but I didn't care about his transgressions or indiscretions. I didn't care that his greed surpassed his morals and that he made a living stealing and cheating. I didn't give one fuck about all the women he messed around with behind his wife's back.

The only thing that I cared about was that in order to achieve all his indiscretions, he needed Tony's help. And Tony wanted payment.

See, if he had done all his business without the need to use Tony, he would have never seen my face, never known my name. But he did. The payment he offered was way too young, too pure, way too broken to ever heal. And I was about to ensure that he too would be a broken man. He was never going to recover from my visit.

Romeo turned off the headlights as we neared the long winding road to the farmhouse. He pulled onto the side road and parked the car. We were going to walk the rest of the way.

The air felt heavy, almost suffocating as it slid into my lungs and imploded in my chest with each breath. I could hear the other men breathing. It was like a singular heartbeat, shallow and uncertain. The men broke apart, slowly we rounded the property and there would be nowhere to run, nowhere to hide.

My heart chugged in my chest when I walked right up to his front door. It was immaculate and white with a brass knocker, and I slammed it again and again until lights came on and Pete himself opened the door. He wore sleep on his face and a stretched greying singlet over blue boxers. His grey whiskers were already growing and his thinning hair gleamed in the porch light.

He squinted, "What the fu..." his words fell away as he recognised me. His breath stank of alcohol.

"May we come in?"

He rubbed his hands over his face, and he staggered a little as he stepped aside letting me walk inside.

"To what do I owe this late night visit?" His voice was scratched with sleep and slurry from alcohol. It was ok. He was about to sober up real quick.

"Where's the rest of your family?"

At that he stuttered, "My family?"

"Where?"

"What are you doing here Gabriel?"

I nodded at Salvatore and the two other men. In a swift movement Salvatore kicked Pete's legs from beneath him and he fell to the ground. A second later cold steel pressed against his temple.

"Where?"

"Up… up… upstairs," he stuttered. "Sleeping."

I turned to Romeo, "Go get them."

"What's this about Gabriel? I thought we were friends? Let's talk about it."

"Keep your mouth shut."

"Gabriel, I don't under…" Salvatore smashed the gun against his temple, and Pete swayed like a reed in the wind then closed his mouth.

We made our way to the lounge area, our heavy boots thumping on the hardwood floor polished and shining against the glaring lights. Salvatore pushed Pete onto the floor. He knelt beside his lavish black, leather couch and hand carved coffee table; intricate designs marking the edges. Nothing in this room seemed accidental; from the ridiculous chandelier to the modern rugs, it all screamed money. A box filled with riches he had amassed on the back of his child.

We listened as feminine voices drifted from upstairs. They soon turned to cries and screams, and a few moments after that Romeo showed up dragging Pete's wife and older son. They both struggled against him, fists swinging against his broad chest. He didn't blink as he hauled them forwards. They froze when they saw us.

"Gabriel?" His wife's surprise was amusing. She walked the rest of the way down on her own, her son following suit. "What's going on?" A silk robe was wrapped around her too perfect body. Her perky tits on display though the slit. She was as opulent as the house, packed full of silicone and botox.

"Just sit down next to your son." Salvatore answered for me.

She gasped as she saw her husband, a small trickle of blood oozed from behind his ear. "Pete? What's going on?"

A hush fell across the room as a reedy girl that was on the cusp of being a teenager walked down the stairs, shadowed by Romeo. He didn't touch her, as instructed. Her nightgown clung to her skeletal body and dark crescents bent below her sunken eyes.

She hesitated on the last stair, and her piercing gaze fell on the scene. I can't imagine how it might have looked to her; five men clad in black, armed and surrounding her family, her bleeding father whimpering on his knees, her begrudged mother sitting on the couch with her son tucked under her arm huddling together.

She trembled as she took unsteady steps and stopped at the door, leaning against the frame, seemingly unafraid. I guess enduring Tony had been her worst nightmare, fear was an acquaintance she had parted with long ago.

"What's going on?" She asked, her voice steady and sure, her eyes boring into mine.

"We've come to teach your father a lesson."

At that she perked up, "Oh? What sort of lesson?"

"That every action has an equal and opposite reaction, and that being in debt will create a deficit that needs to be filled."

"I'm not in debt to anyone! I've paid all my dues." Pete shouted and Salvatore shut him up with a kick to the lower back. He crumpled, squealing. Salvatore and Romeo pulled him back up to his knees.

"But you are in debt Mr. Monroe, to your daughter here."

He swung his gaze to her, his eyes burning with anger.

"What are you talking about?" He hissed through clenched teeth.

I reached into my pocket and pulled out the photograph. The harrowed face of the girl that looked back at me scalded my very soul, it was about to do the same to her father.

I placed the photograph on the coffee table. The room fell silent, like every noise had been sucked out, as if we were suddenly encapsulated in a bubble that had frozen time itself. All eyes roamed the picture, the reactions came all at once.

Romeo swung his head away cursing. Salvatore clenched his jaw, the lines around his eyes tightening, the knuckles on his trigger hand whitening. The mother shrieked and the son pushed away from her, his eyes growing wild as his head swung from his parents to his sister, "What the fuck is this?" He screamed. Pete's eyes fell to the floor looking at nothing. The girl…she looked at the picture as if it wasn't even there, like she was looking at something else. Someone else.

"See, Mr. Monroe, you are in debt to my conscious, to my very soul. To your daughter, who didn't want to be used as payment for sick fucks like Tony." At my words, his wife gasped, tears rolling down her eyes as she looked from her husband to her daughter. Her face transformed, I could see each muscle shift and change as comprehension set in. I bet that in last ten years she had questioned hundreds of times what had happened to her giggly five-year-old girl, where the dancing disappeared to, where the smiles vanished to, where the songs and the life fell away.

She didn't know.

She wouldn't suffer. She would get to keep her fake tits and swollen lips.

"You fucker!" She screamed and leapt from the couch, her fists and palms smashing against her husband's body. He took the beating like a rock in a stormy sea allowing the brutal waves to crash upon it.

She screamed as she smashed herself against him, the son joining in, feeding off her anger. He was not older than fifteen, but he was a farmer and his strong arms were used to hard labour. His shots were brutal.

We stood and watched, allowing them to feel, the hate, to

take it all in. Shivering, the woman ran to her daughter who stepped out of her reach.

"Diana, why didn't you tell me? All these years..." she cried, her body shivered, withering. She reached for the girl again and, again, she moved out of her reach.

"That's enough." I tipped my head to Romeo who pulled the boy away from his father, who lay bleeding in a puddle on the floor. His hands covered his head, blood leaking through his fingers. The boy fought, trying to pry himself away from Romeo's grasp. He screamed and cursed as the bigger man held him.

"Calm down or I'll have to put you down. I have work to do."

The boy clenched his fists and sucked in breath, he steadied himself then stilled. Romeo released him.

I looked to the mother and son, suddenly broken. In an instant they had transformed into new people. "I have work to do here, if you interfere, I will have to punish you too. Do you understand?"

"Yes." She whimpered a cry while the boy nodded, his eyes glazed with hatred as he looked at his father.

"Go upstairs and pack a bag. You will not have a home after tonight," it came out as if I was telling them about the weather.

They both remained where they were.

"Go! Now!"

At that they sprung up and held each other as they climbed the stairs to their rooms.

I turned to the girl who was once again looking at her father. There was no hatred there—or anger. In fact, there was nothing at all. She was empty, the cracks had allowed all her emotions to leak right out of her. Tonight, I was going to help her heal. I was going to glue those cracks shut so that she could be whole again. Feel again.

"Diana?"

She turned to look at me with glassy eyes.

"I have many ideas for the way I would like to punish your father. But do you?"

Tears pooled at the rims of her eyes and her lower lip quivered, the stony exterior she has lived inside, cracking, healing.

Her mouth quavered; words that had been held captive inside her heart wanting to spill out. She wobbled on uncertain feet, approaching me. She was cautious like a deer approaching a predator. I held still waiting. I didn't want to spook her, no sudden movements to make her run.

She stood a hairsbreadth away from me. I could feel her heat, I could see her body shivering; fear, uncertainty, and anger all swarming beneath her skin and behind her eyes.

"No one is ever going to hurt you again." Our eyes locked and I think that she believed me, because her body stilled and her eyes tightened. A calm settled around her as she pushed up to her tiptoes and whispered in my ear.

I nodded, remaining still and allowed her to back away.

"Diana?" Her head tipped upwards, she looked at me through a curtain of dirty blonde hair. "I'm sorry, I—"

She stepped closer and her hand closed around mine, silencing me, "It's ok. I knew one day you would come." Her voice was hoarse and gruff like it hadn't been used in a very long time.

I nodded, words failing me, my apology falling to the ground. She pulled away from me, "Your past is about to burn away, go give yourself a fresh start."

She nodded and walked to the stairs. I want to believe that I saw a little spring of joy in her steps.

"We're going to the barn." I turned around and walked towards the door while Salvatore and Romeo dragged the bleeding, whimpering mess of Pete Monroe, leaving a trail of blood on the exquisite floor.

"Make sure they get out, then burn it down." I looked at

Leo, he nodded then made his way upstairs to hurry them up.

The barn was an impressive structure, like a monument to the livestock that inhabited it. The white walls and red roof stood out like an unwelcome spot on the land. I hauled open the oiled door, expecting resistance. My fingers missed the heavy iron door of the garage, the simplicity of it all.

The smell wrapped itself around me as I walked deeper into the barn. A musty odour of animal fur and the stink of new and dried-out manure. The low grunts of animals and creaking boards drifted through the dim structure. As my eyes grew adjusted to the weak light, I could make out the shapes of the wooden stalls and poles, the equipment and bales of straw and hay piled onto one another.

The ceiling was high with decorative wooden rafters crossing the entire structure. The deeper we walked the worse the smell became.

This would be a good place.

The animals began to stir. They could feel our presence—a scratch against a stall, thumps, grunts—The animals were waking to witness Pete's fall.

When we reached the end of the barn, Salvatore and Romeo released Pete and he fell to the ground.

"Please Gabriel, I can make this all go away." I ignored his pleas, the time for forgiveness was over.

"I'm not the one you should be begging for forgiveness."

"Please…"

"Strip".

His red eyes shot to me in disbelief, "Gabriel."

"Now."

"No! I won't, kill me if you must."

"Pete," I smiled at him and squatted down so that I could grab his chin and lift his face to mine. I looked into his eyes, "I'm not going to kill you. I'm going to make you suffer."

With that, Salvatore lashed out with a brutal kick to his

lower back and he collapsed onto me. I moved away letting his face fall onto the floor with a choked gurgle.

I grabbed a length of rope and we picked Pete's heavy body up, pinning him then securing him against the far stall. We pulled his feet and hands apart, spread eagled. He was going to learn all about vulnerability and accountability.

His eyes focused once more just as my knife sliced through his clothes. His head lolled for a second then snapped backwards smashing into the wall behind him, "Gabriel, what the hell are you doing?"

I ignored him. My knife sliced through his old, faded singlet. It fell open limp and pathetic, much like its owner. His fat, hairy stomach spilt over the elastic of his boxers.

"Do you regret what you did?" I stepped back and looked at him.

"I was building an empire, setting my family up for the future."

I bit my lower lip and tried again, agitation building inside me, "Do you regret what you did?"

"She coped ok, recovered. You saw her."

"Do. You. Regret. What. You. Did?" My jaw clinched as my hand tightened against the knife. I sucked in a breath remembering that killing him would not be punishment enough.

"I was doing it for my family, it was what needed to be done..." his voice fell away as tears brimmed his eyes. But I knew just then that his tears were not for Diana or for her stolen years, her youth and innocence. The tears were for him and him alone, for his growing fear and uncertainty, for watching his black empire crumble. He had no regrets, and I had no shred of sympathy left for this pathetic man.

I turned to Salvatore, "Go find a calf, it's feeding time."

Salvatore remained deadpanned as he turned around and looked through stalls. On the contrary, Pete struggled against his restraints, "What the fuck are you doing Gabriel? Stop this now."

I ignored him and grabbed the elastic of his boxers slicing through the fabric, easily ripping it from him. It fell to below his knees revealing a small shrivelled cock peppered in white hair.

"Gabriel, ok. Yes, I regret what I did. I'm sorry, ok? Gabriel!" His voice strained, and his body wobbled as he tried to fight the rope.

From behind us the thunder of hooves grew as a young calf ran through the barn, suddenly free. His movements began to wake the rest of the animals, but I wasn't worried about them. They were sealed tight—for now.

The calf approached us, obviously used to people. I guess he recognised Pete's smell. It ran around in circles. Pete shuddered each time the calf neared him, rubbing it's head on his naked body. Through the windows the night lit up as orange flames consumed the family home. Light danced on Pete's ashen features as he watched his world collapse around him.

The calf sniffed at Pete who screamed and begged, but now it was all too late. I didn't need to watch the show. I knew what was coming. We all did.

"I had other ideas for you, but when Diana suggested this, I cannot think of anything better that filth like you deserve. You know, you might even enjoy it—if he doesn't suck it off that is."

"Gabriel! Gabriel come back here! Gabriele, you sick fuck, this isn't funny."

The calf approached and smelled the man who was struggling against his restraints, screaming and begging.

"If you ever harm your daughter or anyone ever again, you will not get off so lightly." He wasn't listening, eyeing the calf as it sniffed his body, "Your debt is now paid."

I turned my back to Pete, Salvatore and Romeo flanking

me. His screams followed us down the barn now alive with frothing animals, kicking and mooing.

"No. Get away! No, no, no. No!" Pete squealed, his screams pierced the night that glowed warmly with the inferno now encasing the entire family residence.

Leo escorted the family into a car, and we watched as they drove off. I wasn't worried. No one would ever say what happened here. From behind us came the screams of the tortured man. I wasn't sure if the sudden warmth that filled me was the burning house or the satisfaction.

I turned to Romeo, "Wait thirty minutes then let a few other animals loose."

"When do I cut him down?"

"Don't."

He nodded and looked at his watch. Romeo was a good soldier.

The first of my visits was over, but the night was not nearly done.

I only managed three more visits before dawn. But I was satisfied, knowing out there that these men were getting what they deserved.

In a single night I had washed away their sins and ended their worlds, just as they had done for their children.

Truth was, that night broke me too, something irreparable in my wiring. Because, I enjoyed watching it all burn, watching them break, watching them suffer. Only a monster would feel those things.

Sometimes it still didn't feel like what they got was enough, it never would be—not really. But knowing those men were sodomised and brutalised, stripped of their masculinity, and made to suffer in a way that would break something vital inside of them was a start.

I had been talking for so long that the sun had moved along the horizon. The memories made my stomach churn and my heart beat in a frenzy. I could feel the searing heat of the fire against my skin and Diana's cold, skeletal hands as they wrapped around my own.

I wondered if she ever managed to find peace.

Mia studied me with a mournful expression, the gold flecks in her eyes glinting in her unshed tears. "Gabriel." She shifted closer towards me and allowed me to gather her into my arms. Her soft lips laying a gentle kiss against my neck.

"I would have done the same thing." It was all she said, bringing the matter to a close.

I wanted to have her then on that picnic rug. I wanted her knees to burn with the friction of my body against hers, I wanted the cool winter air to pebble her nipples and her breasts to fall into my hands. I wanted to be buried deep inside her and let the sun bathe our naked bodies with the little heat it held. But somehow, she felt fragile and delicate, and maybe I was too. Which is why I needed her so badly, which is also why I held her and released her and signalled for Max to come back.

I packed up the picnic basket that was mostly untouched. I guess talking about maiming people who hurt kids isn't conducive to an appetite.

"Did you get all of them?"

"Every last one."

She nodded, her eyes focused somewhere far away.

"Mia? Are you ok?"

She nodded again and bit her quivering lower lip. "Mia?"

"I'm fine." She gave me a weak smile.

Before I could say anything more, Max arrived with the horses and helped pack up the rest of the picnic gear. He led us back to the trail and we rode back in silence.

Max dropped us off by the golf cart, and I drove us back to the cabin. We grabbed our stuff and hopped onto the bike.

I could feel Mia. Her silence wasn't empty. It was full of words and thoughts and desires she didn't share with me, and I didn't know how to ask her to. So I remained silent too.

The bike vibrated and screamed beneath us, crushing the silence into melodic metal that sang as it pistoned and worked to move us back to Hill Street.

I parked it underground in my private garage and took the elevator to the lobby.

"I have to see Salvatore."

Mia nodded at me. She still felt far away.

"Mia? Where are you?"

"Go, I'm fine. I'll wait upstairs." I watched as the elevator door shut behind her and she vanished. I exhaled a breath I didn't realise I had been holding. Why the hell was I suddenly walking on eggshells around her?

I drew the door back and stepped into Sin. It was crowded, too crowded. I pushed my way through drunk young men and topless waitresses and stepped into the office. Salvatore looked up and I swore I could see relief wash across his face.

"Happy to see me?"

"Welcome back."

"It was one night." One night that felt both like an eternity and like a split second, "Anything new?"

He looked at the floor and shook his head. "Nothing."

I sighed, the weight of his words bearing down on me. "I guess we're out of options, time to sit down with Lupe."

"I'll arrange it."

"Good."

PART XXI

True to her nature, Alice stayed buried in her deep tunnel. It had been almost six months before she crawled out to attend Simone's funeral and another week till the phone rang, "Hi kiddo."

I paused at the sound of Alice's voice, I can't say it was expected or welcome, "Hi Alice, it's been awhile."

"So good to hear your voice," she sounded melancholy. I had nothing to say. "I'm clean." She went on.

"That's good." I pinched the bridge of my nose wondering what she wanted.

"I'd like to see you…if you wouldn't mind."

"Not sure that's such a good idea Alice."

"Please Kiddo."

"Alice—"

"I just want to talk."

"When?"

"In about an hour? In the usual spot." I hated that she referred to that bench as the 'usual spot'. The usual spot for what? For nights spent freezing while she was passed out on the floor beneath me, gagging or convulsing? The usual spot where men had their hands or dicks in her for chump change? The usual spot she's dragged me when we were kicked out of another place to live.

I exhaled trying to expel all my anger. It didn't work. I looked at my watch and slammed my eyes shut.

"Kiddo?"

"Ok, I guess I can do that. I'll bring some coffee."

"That would be nice." I scoffed at the word. Nice. It felt so bland, such a meagre word to describe our relationship. It was anything but nice. It was barely anything at all. "See you soon." She said.

The line went dead.

I stepped out of the office and found Mia sitting on the couch, her nose in another book. I made a mental note to have some more brought up for her, "I have to go."

"Where?"

I raked a hand through my hair, my face soured with my words, "Alice wants to meet up, she's back."

Mia put her book down and frowned, "What does she want?"

"She didn't say, but I have to go."

"Have to?"

"Need to." I shrugged, still uncertain why that woman had such a fierce hold on me when she was so willing to let me go so often in life.

Mia stood up and studied my face, "Do you want me to come with you?"

My smile was fleeting, "No, I need to do this one by myself. Romeo is going to stay downstairs. Make sure you don't go anywhere without him." I gave her a long, dark look. She squirmed under it and rolled her eyes at me.

"I'll be back soon."

"I guess I'll just be here…waiting."

I closed the distance between us and grabbed her waist slamming it into my body. I captured her mouth in a long, languishing kiss that promised her it was going to be worth the wait.

I released her breathless and wanting and stepped into the elevator.

I crossed the lobby and climbed on my bike, my skin crawling with apprehension. What did Alice want?

I parked at the edge of the park, where nature tried to reclaim what was hers and humanity forced her inside a cage surrounded by concrete.

I spotted the coffee cart and ordered two coffees, remembering that Alice didn't drink any sugar. I watched the naked trees, the branches swinging aimlessly in the cool breeze. I pulled my jacket tighter around me. A bearded man called my name and handed me the two take away cups. I spotted the doughnuts then and grabbed one—just in case. She may be clean, but she might also be broke.

I stepped into the park, onto the evergreen grass, my body twisting in knots. As much as I hated this place it has always felt like it was a part of me. Or maybe I was an extension of it —a branch that kept losing its leaves then sprouting new ones, at the mercy of the changing seasons. Or maybe, it was just because nothing good ever happened here. Not really.

I spotted Alice on the bench, her restless fingers fidgeting, locking and unlocking, touching invisible things. She kept looking around but she didn't seem scared, more nervous or excited. It was odd. I swallowed my doubts and crept closer, trying to prolong the distance. Alice put on weight again, and her skin looked healthier. Even from this far away, it looked like she was wearing a new shirt—or a clean one at least.

I sucked in a deep breath and crossed the path, "Hi Alice."

"Hey kiddo." She smiled up at me as she pulled a cigarette from a box. She lit up, sucking on the thin stick—the end burning orange—then blew out a long trail of white smoke that hung in the air between us, like all the things that we pretend neither of us saw and then got whisked away by a sudden gust. My lips pressed together in a thin line, and I collapsed into the bench next to her. Disappointment sitting between us like an uninvited guest.

I handed her the coffee and a doughnut. She grabbed both, "Thanks."

"What do you want Alice?"

"Straight to business, hey?"

"I don't have much time."

"For me, you mean?" I pretended I didn't hear her and looked towards my bike, wishing I was heading back to Mia. "Don't be like that kiddo." She patted my thigh and I tried not to shudder. I didn't feel the same.

"I've missed you." She flashed me a wane smile.

I scoffed at her, "Missed me?'

"Sure, sure." She took another drag.

"Fuck you Alice. Missed me? Is that cause you sobered up for five minutes? We both know, a month from now, a year from now, that you're gonna go back on the heroin…or cocaine, or whatever the fuck you find that gives you the highest high or the most surreal escape. You're going to forget about me all over again. But guess what Alice? I'm not a kid anymore, and you can't just drop me off with another Tony or some other fucker that'll stick his fingers up your twat for fifty bucks. If you want money, just ask. But don't just drop back into my life and feed me this shit." My face felt hot and my hands shook. I tucked them into my pockets, digging my nails into my palms. The pain helped to draw my emotions.

Alice sucked on her cigarette, her face drawn. The smoke cascaded from her mouth with a long sigh, "Guess I deserved that, but I didn't leave you alone."

"What do you call dropping me off at Tony's?"

"I left you with family."

My body felt rigid, my muscles tightening and straining against my skin, "What the fuck are you talking about?"

"I left you with your brother."

Adrenaline pumped everywhere and drowned out everything as I tried to understand what she was saying to me, "What are you talking about Alice?"

Her brown doe eyes locked with mine, "You might've had a different father, but you and Salvatore share a mother." Her mouth tipped upwards in one corner, "The one big difference between you was that his father wanted to keep him and your father didn't," Her hands flew to her mouth and her eyes grew wide. She tried to reach for me but I filched away, "That wasn't what I meant to say."

But it was too late. I got it, I was damaged goods. Even as a kid no one fucking wanted me. My ears pounded as my veins flooded with heat, "Why the fuck didn't you tell me before?"

"I thought you guys would figure it out by now, you have so many things in common." She shrugged and dragged that fucking cigarette.

"We have nothing in common!" I roared at her.

"You do." She sat non-pulsed and scratched the end of her cigarette butt on the sole of her shoe, extinguishing the ember. She looked at me again and there was that smile, sad and pathetic. I wanted to erase it from her face, to take it away forever, but I also wanted some fucking answers, "I've never told Salvatore because I wasn't allowed to. That was his father's choice, his rules. It was just part of the deal," she shrugged, "I had to keep away from him, so I watched him from afar. But, I knew he was going to watch over you."

"I can't believe you kept this from me!" It was a low whisper and, for the first time, she flinched.

"Kiddo, I tried."

"Yes Alice, that's all you've ever done. You've tried and failed, again and again and again!"

"Gabriel, don't say that."

"What else do you want me to say? I have forgiven you time and time again, but I've been alone for so long. I've been so broken, and all this time I could have—"

"You could have what?" She cut me off. "Do you think if you knew he was your brother he would've treated you any differently? Would it have made that much of a difference? He was working for Tony, that wouldn't have changed. Anyway, look at you. You run this business of yours together, you spend more time with him than anyone else does. The fact that you're related by blood makes no difference."

I dragged a hand through my hair, my teeth grinding. Maybe that's why Alice was so broken, she never understood the value of family. The power of it.

"It makes all the fucking difference." I hissed at her.

"Yeah?" She grabbed the coffee and took an excruciatingly long sip, as if we were talking about traffic or insurance policies. My body shook and my jaw screamed with tension. "I'm done apologising Gabriel, I've apologised enough times. It's now time to make amends. I can't do this with you anymore. I know I failed, I know I've screwed up more than once. And you know what? I might screw up again, but *this* is my last apology." Her eyes focused on mine and her back straightened, "I did what I did, what I could to survive. It wasn't always good enough; hell, most of the time it wasn't good at all, but it was all that I could do," her hand reached for me, and I flinched away again. Her lips stretched in a thin line across her face, and that stupid smiled of hers tilted downwards, "I was young and stupid and lost. I was on drugs, and that was the only escape I had. I know you think you're the only one who suffered, but I had to make sacrifices too and I did. For you. You might not have seen it, but I did what I could with what I had and you just have to accept that."

Her face twisted as if she had sucked on a lemon, then brightened as if the sun had come up inside of her, "You may not feel like I loved you, but *you* were the biggest treasure in my life. You're still the one thing that always keeps me anchored, rooted. The one thing that makes me want to try harder and be better."

"What about your other son?" I snapped. I shouldn't have, but anger coursed through my veins. It was all too late, too much. I wasn't going to let her off the hook because she finally remembered to say she loved me.

"I wish things were different." Was all she said. Alice pulled another cigarette from her pack and smoked silently. Like a puffing dragon, she sat beside me and her words dripped into me like an IV filled with poison—slowly spreading through my veins, to the insides of my body, coating every muscle, every tendon, and all the pieces of my flesh like a drug. It made me dizzy.

I had a brother.

Salvatore.

I should have been elated, and maybe for a few seconds I was—the highest of highs. My heart strummed and my world expanded. In mere minutes it had grown exponentially for another whole human that, in some ways, belonged to me and I belonged to them. For a second I might have even loved Alice for telling me, but that was the effect of the drug she fed me. See, with the highest high comes the lowest low, and just as quickly as I flew, I plummeted back to my reality.

Having family came with a price. Salvatore would become another person that could be used against me—a weapon, a crack. He was a good man, he'd always been good to me. But what would he become now? I suddenly felt like he was so much more.

"Does he know?"

"I don't know." She shrugged, and I wanted to rattle her small body and break it.

"I have to go Alice, I'll see you around." She grabbed my arm before I could get up.

"Gabriel," her eyes were fierce and teary, her worn face looked old and worried like all the years had finally caught up with her, "I should've told you sooner, I'm sorry."

I snapped my hand away and turned to walk away.

"Gabriel?" She called me again, "Can you come back next month? Maybe the last Friday? I'll be here, if you say you'll come. We can talk and catch up, you can tell me how you are and I'll try harder."

"I don't think so Alice." I hissed through gritted teeth.

"Please?"

I didn't know if I wanted to see Alice again, I didn't know how I felt just then. All I knew was that I had a brother, and I wanted to find out what he knew. I didn't turn around as I made my way back to my bike and tore down the road, back to Hill Street—my heart hammering.

I barged into the office, slamming the door against the back wall and rushing in like a blistering wind. "Did you know?" Salvatore looked up at me from a pile of papers, his face twisted in surprise as I rounded the table and yanked him out of the chair, pinning him against the wall, "Did you know?"

"Did I know what?" He grabbed my wrist looking into my eyes, his burning with fury.

"Do you know who your mother is?"

"I don't know a fucking thing about my mother or who she is. My dad never talked about her. Said she was a piece of trash that left me, and didn't want anything to do with us." I let him go, his body sliding against the wall. He straightened his shirt and shoved me, the force knocking me over the table. I stumbled backwards and corrected, staring into his vicious stare. "Why the fuck are you asking me about my mother?"

I rubbed my hands over my face, not knowing how to start. But I had already opened the can of squirming, rotting worms and there was no putting them back in. I exhaled then started, "I know who your mother is."

Salvatore took a step closer, his expression darkening, "How the fuck could *you* possibly know who my mother is?"

"Because I met her today."

"You? Met her?" He took another step, his fists clenched at his sides, "Then why the fuck did you attack me, and who the fuck is this mysterious woman?"

"Alice."

Salvatore froze at the mention of the name.

"Alice? As in *your* Alice?"

"As in *our* Alice, it seems." I cleared my throat as if trying to dislodge the ugly truth from it.

Salvatore's brow crinkled like an old newspaper and his mouth opened and closed a number of times before he finally found his voice again, "Are you saying that we are…"

"That's how it seems."

"You must be fucking joking, I can't be related to your ugly face"

"You know what? That's exactly the first thing I thought too."

He landed back into the chair, the fight leaching away from his body. His brow dug in and he raked his hands through his hair, "You sure?"

I shrugged, "I'm not sure of much that Alice says or does. Your guess is as good as mine. I guess we can do a DNA test if you want to "

"Does it make a difference to you?" He looked at me and I saw something there, or at least I hoped I did—those same hidden feeling I shut behind my eyes. The feeling of wanting to belong. To be part of something bigger than myself. Mia was a start, a beginning of expanding my heart, my legacy, and my family. Salvatore could be another limb; a strong branch that will be attached to my roots forever. He would be dependent on my survival in the same way that I would be dependent on his.

The truth was yes, I wanted that fucking DNA test more than anything. But anything that can be snapped off makes you weak. I can be a solitary tree, withstand the winds and blizzards and weather. I'd be worn and beat up but I'd be alive. But start snapping off my branches, and I'd experience pain and loss so deep I may never recover. Thing was, Salvatore was already so much like a brother that making it official would only give him a new title. *Brother.* I shrugged again, "Would it really change anything?"

His lips pressed together in a slight grimace, holding back the truth, "I guess not."

"Well then, let's find that fucker, Emilio Rocco, and finish this. We need to protect our family's business."

At my words Salvatore's eyes flinched to mine, and we remained locked in a stare that, like hundreds of times before, shared all the words neither of us ever spoke. I looked away first, my heart stuttering.

Salvatore let out a long breath, that seemed to fill the room with a heavy uncertain silence.

"So," he spoke at last, a slow smile creeping across his features, "What now? Do I call you bro instead of boss?"

"Please don't call me either, you know I hate it when you do that."

"Yes, I do boss," he said it with the slight curl of his lips, breaking into a full smirk, "Now that I've got a little brother, I guess I can torment him."

"How's that any different to what you've been doing to me for the last ten years?"

Salvatore chuckled, "Call me sentimental."

"More like senile."

"You might be my little brother, but remember I can still kick your ass."

"Used too."

He squared his shoulders and straightened his spine, "Is that a challenge little bro?"

I rolled my eyes, already getting tired of this new little taunt he has found, "To be tabled until we finish off our real business."

"To be continued then."

He ran his hands over his face and the mirth fell away as he pulled his chair in and bent over the desk.

"I'm going upstairs to break the news to Mia."

Salvatore gave me one of his blank looks and shifted his attention to his work as I left the room.

I burst through the elevator doors and called for Mia. I was greeted with silence. "Mia?" I called out to her and searched the penthouse, tearing from room to room like a hurricane.

The penthouse was empty. I could feel the anger as it flowed through my veins like hot lava, pushing its way to the surface and waiting for just the right moment to explode.

Where the fuck was Mia.

I had no patience for the elevator and leapt like an escaped mad man down the emergency staircase. Heat pulsed in my head and my fingers shook as I searched for Mia. For Romeo.

When I found him, he was tits deep in Emery—the German stunner leaning against the wall, allowing him to suck one of her dark nipples while her long black hair covered the other. Her piercing green eyes were shut and she let out a soft moan as Romeo bit lightly then sucked her back into his mouth.

Romeo would never finish his exploits of Emery's tits because I yanked him by the collar and smashed him against the wall. Emery shrieked, her eyes flying open and her hands flying to her breasts covering herself.

I smashed Romeo's head into the wall twice more before I turned to Emery.

"Go back to work."

She didn't say a word as she scurried away, leaving a moaning Romeo pinned against the wall, a small trail of blood above his right eye where the broken plaster had cut him.

"Boss—"

"Where the fuck is Mia?"

"She went out boss."

"Out?" I growled through clenched teeth, and Romeo flinched as our noses almost touched, "And why are you not out with her?"

"I was for a while, but then she said something about wanting to surprise you and…"

I didn't hear the rest of his words, they sounded too familiar already. A surprise. Didn't she say something about a surprise the day Simone died? Didn't she vanish that day too?

I bit my lip and tuned back in, "…Sorry boss." He was whimpering.

"I guess you thought you might find her all over Emery's tits, did you?"

He opened and closed his mouth a few times, then choose wisely and said nothing at all.

"Find Mia. Let me know as soon as you do." I hissed at him through a haze of fury, my knuckles shaking at his chest.

"Yes boss."

"Fix this shit." I smashed him against the dent in the wall once more and let him drop from my grasp. He wobbled and brought his hand to his sliced eyebrow. "And clean yourself up too."

"Yes boss."

He stared at me for another few seconds.

"Go!" I roared at him, and he took off towards the exit.

I could barely breathe, the air seemed to compress around me. Spots bounded by my feet as I stared out of the window, wondering where she could be and why she would disobey me again. Fire burned inside of me, a fury so hot I didn't know I could feel it so deeply, so strongly, so intensely. The fire burned me up from the inside out, my sanity dripping away like sweat.

I paced the apartment, Spots running circles around the couch, his tongue hanging from his mouth. He seemed as restless as I felt, "Sorry buddy, I'll take you out as soon as I know where Mia is."

As the sound of her name, he bounded up excited, "I know buddy, I feel that way too. But she's not here…"

I scratched the bald spot behind his ear, the hard skin moving like rubber beneath my fingers. His tail smacked the ground as I patted him. His face swivelled to my office a nanosecond before the phone rang, and he bounded to the door as if the call was for him.

I grabbed the receiver and put it to my ear, "It's me." Disappointment washed over me at the sound of Salvatore's voice and my heart, which has been beating in a frenzy, squeezed in my chest.

"What is it?"

"Lupe has agreed to a sit down."

"When?"

"He'll be here in thirty minutes."

I looked at my watch and pinched the bridge of my nose.

"Fine. Conference room three." I hung up.

I showered. I don't know why. Maybe the mention of his name made me feel dirty, or maybe any association to him felt like it dug out the past that I wanted to keep buried. His name alone took me for a stroll through my murky soul.

I dressed, a tailored suit that fitted me perfectly. I don't know why I felt like I had to put on this show. Maybe I wanted to shove in his face how far we'd come. The brave twenty-one-year-old that that had nothing had built an empire that even his bosses couldn't touch. *Wouldn't* touch.

I sat at the head of the table, my fingers laced in front of me. My shoulders square, my face vacant. Tension coursed through my veins thicker than blood and I was doing all I could not to choke on it. Mia's disappearance gnawed at me, and meeting up with Lupe reeked of desperation. He knew it just as much as I did, but I wasn't going to give him an inch.

Lupe's eyes locked on mine the second he rounded the corner. Salvatore flanked him, leading him down the corridor. The floor to ceiling glass was the only thing separating us. The door swung open and let out a breath of stale air, then closed behind us sealing us inside—like a secret.

His feline eyes narrowed as he sat down, his face pulled in a smirk.

I tried not to breath, not to flinch, schooling my features —holding everything at bay, ordering every muscle to relax and every tendon to loosen up. I waited for him to settle into the chair. His blonde hair had thinned out. Still meticulously combed, the once thick locks now pathetic strands.

"Well, well, well, as I live and breath. The great Gabriel D'Angelo asked to see me." He started with his smarmy voice, mocking me in my home.

I didn't bite. "Lupe."

He looked around the conference room and whistled as he took in the leather chairs, polished wooden floors, and long glass table that stretched across the room.

"To what do I owe this displeasure?"

To his credit, he hadn't changed a bit.

"Thank you for coming."

"Well, when someone in your position asks to see someone like me, I can't really refuse can I?" He stretched his hands and splayed his palms across the cold glass table. He was missing both pinkies and two other fingers from his left hand.

I pretended not to notice, although we both knew that I had. But I wasn't there to play his games, or take his bait. The only reason he was there was to give me information, nothing more.

"I need information."

"You need help." A slimy smile slid across his face.

"Not yours."

"Well seems to me I've wasted my time." He made to get up.

"Sit down," I bellowed, my brow creased, my composure cracking. Salvatore pushed Lupe back into the chair. His smile grew bigger and I sucked in a long calming breath.

"Help and information are two different commodities, which are therefore valued differently. What I need, and will pay for, is information. What I do not need, nor want from you, is help of any kind."

Lupe's face twisted in a wicked smile, "Call it what you want D'Angelo, either way you'll have to pay up."

"What do you want?"

He watched Salvatore as he spoke, "The redhead from the bar. I want her to suck my dick."

The lines around Salvatore's eyes tightened, "We're not that kind of place."

"It doesn't matter." He leaned back into his seat and laced his hands behind his head.

"I can't force a woman to do that."

"Who said anything about forcing? I'm sure if Mr. Delluci over there flashed her one of his smiles and asked her real nicely, she would do just about anything for him."

I turned to Salvatore. His eyes had darkened, his face full of hatred, "Go get Amber."

"Are you fucking kid—"

"Go get Amber. Now."

Salvatore stormed out of the room, thundering down the corridor, "Your buddy over there doesn't seem happy. Does he have a hard on for her or something?" Lupe cackled.

"He'll do what he's told."

"Yes, he will. Salvatore has always been a very good dog. Speaking of which, how is your mutt?"

"He has a very good memory."

That shut him up for a few seconds.

"I want to know about Emilio Rocco."

"Why?"

"That's none of your business."

He shifted in his chair and scratched at his collar. His suit seemed cheap, used even. Whatever they were using Lupe for these days, he was not in the higher ups. His fuck up with me would have cost him his rank. To be honest, I was surprised it didn't cost him his life.

The more I studied the man, the more I realised that he would not be able to help me at all, and he knew that too. A drop of dread sank into my heart and soon it had pumped it around my body, creating a toxic concussion of unease and apprehension.

"This meeting is over." I stood up.

"So soon? What about my payment?" He didn't move.

"Why are you here?"

"What do you mean?"

I bent over the table, I put my face to his until I could feel his breath on my mouth, "You know what I mean, why are you here?"

"Because you called."

"The truth." I growled.

"Truth is Gabriel, I'm just the messenger."

"Tell me."

"Not before I get my cock sucked by a beautiful girl while your loyal dog Salvatore watches." He bared his teeth in a twisted grin.

I clenched my jaw.

Salvatore barged back into the room, alone.

"Where's Amber?"

"No one has seen her for a couple of hours." He looked relieved, but his voice held a tremor I've never heard before.

Worry. Salvatore didn't get worried. Unless…

I turned back to my guest.

"Guess you'll have to take a rain cheque."

"Well then, so will you."

Before he could stand up, my hand curled around his scrawny neck and his mocking eyes dimmed, but they weren't scared. He seemed almost relieved. "Who sent you?"

"I'll settle for the dark haired one. The one with the big tits, I bet she can suck a cock real well."

"Who sent you?"

"It doesn't matter, it's too late. For both of us." He cackled.

"Who?"

"Our mutual friend."

"He's no friend of mine." I squeezed his throat, his breathing became more shallow.

Lupe gurgled, his eyes gleamed with mirth at my words.

"Where can I find him?"

"I don't know."

"Don't fuck with me Lupe," I warned, my hands tightening around his throat, his eyes beginning to pop.

"There was only one man who knew where Emilio is, but you got rid of him." Lupe's eyes shone.

"Stephano?"

"Ding, ding, ding. But, you fucking killed him you idiot." Lupe started to laugh, a maniacal screeching thing that stank of desperation.

I caught a glimpse of Romeo as he ran towards the door and pushed it open, "I've got her."

"Keep her there, I'll come find you." He nodded and left; I turned my attention back to Lupe.

"Trouble in paradise?"

"Mind your own business." I growled in his face, and he smirked in mine.

I clenched my jaw, my show of indifference long gone, "The message? What is it?"

"You're fucked, that's what it is." He laughed as I released his throat and exchanged a look with Salvatore.

"Cut him loose. He's no use to us. I have other business to attend to."

Lupe reached for my hand, "You can't cut me loose, Gabriel."

"He needs to go. Now." I looked at Salvatore, who was already walking towards the crumpled man. Lupe fell at my feet and grabbed at my suit pants.

"Don't let me go, just kill me please. Don't send me back."

"This meeting is over." I burst through the glass door and made my way to the elevator bank, Lupe's screaming drowned out by the thick glass walls.

If my thoughts were not so consumed by Mia, if my heart wasn't anchored so deeply in hers, I would have seen it all sooner and clearer. Maybe, just maybe, things would have turned out differently. But I was lost and blind and totally deranged by the time I found Romeo again.

***

"Where the hell is she?"

"In there." Romeo indicated, jumping up and down on the balls of his feet. It was his giveaway—his body couldn't help but twitch whenever he knew he fucked up. He knew there would be repercussions. He gave me a nervous smile, maybe he thought he redeemed himself. My eyes skimmed over the scratch above his eye, I wanted to tear it open and let it bleed all over the tiled floor.

But first, Mia.

I barged into the changing room.

Mia stood towards the back of the room, giggling with Amber. Her shoulder leaning against a locker. Their laughter died down when they saw me. Amber's hand shot to her naked breasts and her smile vanished.

"Out! Now."

"Gabriel…" Mia started. I shot her a look that silenced her, and my gaze pivoted to Amber.

"Now!" I smashed my fist on a nearby locker, my knuckles clanged against the metal, reverberating off the narrow white walls and echoed like thunder in the room. "Wait outside this door, don't move!"

Amber grabbed a shirt and scampered out of the room, looking at her feet, remaining silent.

I slammed the door behind her and clicked the lock into place, uncertain if I was locking us inside or the rest of the world outside. I stalked deeper into the cool room, Mia retreated.

"Where the fuck have you been Mia?" It came out as a long crazed growl.

"I've been out with Amber."

"And you ditched Romeo again?"

"Well…"

"I. Told. You. I need to know where you are at all times." I struggled to get the words out, my jaw locked together in a crushing clench.

"And I told you, I am my own person." She folded her arms across her chest and tried to be brave, but her voice quivered and she took another step backwards.

I crept further into the room, my nostrils flared and teeth ground till I could almost taste powder in my mouth, like I was licking fine gravel, "Did I not *explain* myself to you clearly enough?"

"Gabriel…"

"I fucking *own* you. *You* belong to *me*. You are my prop-

erty and therefore I must know where you are at *all* times."
Heat rose through me and I clenched my fists at the side of
my body.

"I'm not your fucking prisoner Gabriel."

"No. But I'm yours."

We were going to be cellmates in the prison we had
crafted for one another. Although I knew all too well what
that felt like, I didn't care. Mia would have to learn to love
the bars and bare walls she had built with her choices. There
was only one way to protect her, and that was to put this
beautiful bird into my gilded cage. She could have everything
in the world, except for what she really wanted—fresh air,
the ability to be her own person, and freedom.

That was the price she was going to pay for loving me
and it would eat at her each day, like peeling layers of flesh
until she would be reduced to nothing but bones.

Her back touched the far locker and she had run out of
room to retreat, "What are you talking about?" She cleared
her throat.

"You have taken my heart and sealed it in a vault somewhere inside of you. I cannot function without my heart."

"Gabriel—"

I cut her off, "I cannot work, or think, or concentrate, or
fucking breathe not knowing where you are—where my
fucking heart is. Each time you disappear, you are killing me
slowly."

"I'm sorry." She stammered.

"I don't give a fuck about your sorry." I slammed into her
with my body, pinning her against the locker. Her ass
smashed into the metal, setting off another chain reaction of
angry clangs. "Now, tell me where the fuck you went and
what the fuck you were doing."

I loomed over her, her large eyes looking into mine. My
entire body tight and angry.

"I just went out with Amber."

My hand slapped the locker by her ear and the angry metallic boom resonated through us both, "Try again."

"I was with Amber."

My hand slid around her throat, "Where?"

"Gabriel..."

"Where?" I growled. I sounded like a crazed beast, starved and demented.

"Here, I was down here with Amber the whole time."

"Why?"

"Gabriel..."

"Why?"

"I just needed girl time."

"I told you," I breathed in her ear, "Do not go anywhere without Romeo. I can't protect you if I don't know where you are."

"I already have a shadow, I don't need another one." Her eyes slanted into slits.

"You will do what I say."

"Or else?"

"Or I will have to punish you Mia."

"I need to be free Gabriel."

"You gave that up when you said you loved me." Her eyes flashed with anger.

"I was just trying to surprise you."

"I don't like surprises."

"I thought you might like this one." She bit her lower lip.

Something pinged at the back of my brain and crawled its way to the forefront of my thoughts, "You said something about a surprise when Simone died."

"Yes." She wrapped her hands around my waist as my fingers closed around her throat. I wasn't going to soften. Rage rumbled through me, a brewing storm of uncontrolled fury.

"Tell me."

"Punish me." She challenged.

I growled at the huskiness of her voice, "Don't distract me Mia. Tell me."

"No." She licked her lower lip and glared at me.

My hand plunged into her hair and pulled her head back forcefully, exposing her neck, causing her back to arch, "You want to be punished Mia?"

"Mmm hmm."

I ripped her shirt from her body, the tattered material falling like broken wings on either side of her and gasped at her naked torso. I scratched a long finger from her neck to her nipple leaving a long red, angry mark in my wake and pinched her already hardening nipple. I wasn't gentle or kind. I was angry and desperate. She groaned at the touch, feeding my anger.

I tightened my grip on her hair and yanked hard, forcing her back to arc more her hips against mine. Mia was caged against the cold metal. I stretched her to her limits; her body fighting my grip. She wavered, unbalanced against the wall, my hips, and her tip toes her only anchors.

I dipped my mouth to her breast and took her nipple between my teeth, tugging and releasing, pinching and biting, rolling and sucking; until her moans became whimpers and I could feel her pushing into me, her body begging for more. Until the dusky tips of her nipples were tight, throbbing peaks that quivered as I neared them.

"Tell me Mia." I pinched—pulling, rolling, hurting.

"No." She whimpered against me. I snarled.

I grabbed her shoulder and, in a smooth harsh motion, flipped Mia around and crashed her body into the locker. It slammed and clanked in a rumble like thunder clouds before the storm. She gasped at cold metal as it licked her skin. I pinned her body with mine giving her no way to move, caging her with my taught muscle and broad shoulders. My hand slipped into her underwear and found her wet pussy. She groaned at my touch as I flicked my fingers across her. I could feel the tension mount in all her muscles. Her legs stiffened and her back tightened, her hips tried to push and grind against me. I locked her in place—teasing, swiping, flicking, and skimming. My fingers exploring inside her, along her soft delicate wetness, all around that one place her body was begging me for.

"Tell me Mia." I barked.

"Gabriel."

My hand slipped out of her underwear and the hand in the hair yanked forcefully, pulling her torso away from the lockers and against my chest. My hand returned to her nipples, now cold and hard. She groaned as I tormented her endlessly, until her legs quivered and her whimpers became helpless mewls.

"Tell me."

"I wanted to surprise you." Her voice was breathy and uneven as she struggled to speak, my assault on her nipples unrelenting, agonising, torturous pain and devastating pleasure.

"She was teaching me to dance," she sucked in a breath, "For you."

My breath hitched but my hand did not fall away, instead I intensified my assault, pinching harder and rolling unmercifully, teasing until she was ready to shed tears.

"Apologise Mia."

"For what?"

"For disobeying me."

"Gabriel."

My hand plunge back into her underwear and she whined like a broken thing, "Gabriel please." I flicked my fingers around her, grazing, trailing, circling—start, stop, stroke. "Gabriel please."

"I don't want you to beg, I want you to apologise." My scratched voice hoarse. I wanted to finish her, to be buried inside her, her quivering body a desperate invitation.

"I'm sorry Gabriel."

"For?"

She moaned as I pulled my hands away again.

"For disobeying you."

I waited.

"I belong to you, and I will never disappear again."

"Good girl." She had apologised, but she still asked to be punished—and punished she was going to be.

I ripped at my jeans, my hand never leaving her hair. My body still pinned her in place. My hard cock sprang out of its confines and I bend down guiding myself inside her.

I pounded into her, unrelenting. With each pound of my hips the lockers clanged and crashed, and soon I had created a thunderstorm so fierce I could feel the electricity travel through me like lightning. The noise clapped and rumbled around us as the violent storm ripped through me. Until the sky opened up and I came inside her, violent and angry. She moaned her disappointment, her throbbing need unanswered.

When I was done, I ripped myself away from her and tucked myself back in, "Final warning Mia, next time I won't be so kind. Now stay here till I tell you otherwise."

She was still glued to the lockers when I stormed out of the room. Amber stood by the door looking at her feet. Her small shirt barely reaching her waist line.

"Look at me."

She lifted her head, her eyes darting from me to the wall and back again.

"Where were you?" I growled at her.

"Just a quick coffee and then we hung around here." Amber looked sacred. I must have looked the animal I felt I was.

"Go get yourself cleaned up and take the rest of the week off."

"But…"

"Full pay, and I'll tell Salvatore." As she turned to leave, I grabbed her arm, "Tell Mia to get ready for her dance. Romeo will escort her to Sin in ten minutes."

She nodded and scampered back into the change rooms.

I found Romeo standing at the end of the corridor, he had a knowing look on his face that fell as he saw mine. "Next time you lose her will be the last. I want her at Sin in ten minutes, I don't give a fuck if she tells you she's ready or not, you get her there."

"Yes boss."

"Ten minutes." I growled at him

I didn't stick around to hear his excuses.

I stormed into Sin and barged into the office; Salvatore sat with his head in his palms still looking over paperwork.

"Amber was with Mia." A chunk of worry seemed to fall from his heavy shoulders, "Now, close Sin and get everyone out."

"But…"

"Now!"

"Gabriel, whatever personal shit you—"

I didn't let him finish the sentence before I closed the distance between us and ploughed him into the wall, the air cascaded from his lungs in a thud. I pushed against him, our eyes locked and my breathing heavy and shallow. My eyes bored into his, "Now."

He clenched his jaw, holding whatever rebuke he had and tipped his head. The conversation was over.

I released him and he straightened his jacked and raked a hand through his hair, flaying me with a look of distain as he left the office to go shut down Sin.

Ten minutes later I sat in front of the stage, looking at the empty space. The dimmed lights made the large space feel small. Intimate.

The darkness was sliced by yellow light as Romeo

escorted Mia inside. He urged her on as she reluctantly walked inside wearing a robe and an angry expression.

I looked to Romeo, "Wait outside."

He nodded and left the club, leaving only Mia and myself inside.

The darkness engulfed everything but the stage, where a solitary beam shone on a pole.

"How do you feel, luce mia?"

"Fuck you, Gabriel."

I sneered at her, "Get on stage."

"Gabriel—"

"Show me your dance."

"Gabe—"

"Now Mia." I was losing patience. I could feel the crackle of anger as it flared in my palms and danced across my fingers. My hand itched to close around her neck, to hurt, to plough into something beautiful. I needed a distraction—a beautiful, seductive distraction to make me forget how angry I was with her, how frustrated, how needy and broken. She's ruined me, my body frayed with tension and worry.

She pouted like an angry kid, her face still heated and flushed. Her hair a frenzied mess that fell across her shoulders. Mia threw off her robe and stomped up to the stage. She was wearing a crisp button up shirt that reached just below her ass. My stomach coiled at the sight of her.

I turned my back on her and strolled to the back of the bar then poured myself a whisky, my movements purposefully slow. The ice tinkled in the silent space.

"Dance Mia."

Her lip curled out, "I need music."

I reached for the radio and pushed play. A low, slow melody rumbled around the room.

I strolled back to the seat in front of the stage and sat down, nursing the glass in my hand.

Mia stood under the beam unmoving, unperturbed, and totally fucking irresistible.

I waited knowing my resolve was endless, knowing I have played this game before—eventually everyone broke for me. Mia would break too.

I waited. She glowered at me.

I waited. She shifted.

I waited. Her hips began to sway. My lips flickered and my heart stuttered as her body followed suit.

Stiff at first, unsure. A trickle of uncertain movements as her arms reached for the pole and her hips questioned themselves.

Mia swayed, her body elegant and fluid, her confidence growing with each note and each movement. As her hips rolled, she traced the shape of her body below the shirt, her lower lip tucked into her mouth. Her arms left her body and gained even more confidence. Her eyes set alight as bit by bit her inhibitions shredded away.

All her curves moved slowly in perfect harmony, like a river after the rain—full and powerful. The music guided the current of her dance, cadence coursing through her veins, extinguishing all her reservation. Mia ground against the poll, her body telling its own story, as she ripped through the buttons and shed the shirt to the floor, like old skin. Left only in a sparkling set of matching lingerie, I gasped and my cock twitched at the sight of her.

Liberated, she moved gracefully, her body tearing through the empty space around her, tracing invisible lines, seducing, mesmerising. Her body bent and twisted as she broke me down with her passion. She was a tempestuous gale bringing a vicious violent angry storm, and I the fool, who didn't seek shelter in time, was drenched in her.

Our eyes met and I felt all her anger as it flooded through her body and into mine. Her hands snaked behind her back, pulling at the strap of her glittering bra. My hard cock pushed against my jeans, cramped, swollen, and hungry. My breath stalled—

The door flew open and Mia froze as Salvatore barged into Sin, the door casting a long sombre white light against the club.

I swivelled towards him ready to rain blows on his face.

"Boss, trouble. Come now."

I shot a look to Mia, "We're not done! Upstairs now!"

She mumbled under her breath and grabbed the shirt from the floor, wrapping herself in it, scalding me with a pissed off look. My gaze followed to the door, "You best be waiting for me when I'm done with this."

She flipped me the bird and walked out to the back passage. If Salvatore wasn't standing at the door I might have gone after her and broken it off. I pushed the thought aside. There was time to break pieces of Mia later.

I bolted from the room. Thoughts of Mia hung on my mind—unfinished, undone. Just like me.

I stormed out of Sin, following Salvatore, his back straight, his posture stiff, his jaw set in an angry scowl.

"Salvatore?" I tried to ask as we tore through the lobby and made our way into the back passages of Hill Street. A hidden labyrinth that connected each room and each space and a few escape routes.

He ignored me and kept marching.

He pushed through the door to the loading dock. The open space, usually bustling with trucks and loaders, was eerily quiet. We walked though the room, containers and boxes littered the concrete floor. I followed Salvatore towards the office tucked away in the far left corner.

I spotted the three men. Romeo and Leo were standing over a bleeding man. When I edged closer, I saw it was Joey. His face had been beaten into a pulpy mess. His eyes swollen, his face almost unrecognisable. His breathing was shallow and strained, he wheezed as he tried to force air into his broken body.

"Get him to a hospital." I hissed, heat rising to my face as fresh fury surged through my veins.

Romeo pulled him up and escorted him into a waiting car. He placed Joey in the front seat, his head lolling, his blood smearing across the windows and interior. They drove off, tyres screeching tired leaving behind a puff of exhaust smoke.

I turned my attention to Leo. His face was swelling and his lower lip cut. I ventured a guess that his body would look much the same—red and angry.

"What happened?"

"We were over run, we couldn't stop them."

"Them who?"

"I don't know. It all happened so fast, we barely got out."

I turned to Salvatore, "Car, now." But he was already running out of the loading dock, his heavy steppes echoing in the large chamber.

"Did they say anything?"

Leo shook his head and brushed a hand over his face, twitching as his sweaty palm swiped his swollen lip, "I don't think so."

"Get someone to look at you." He tipped his head, and I smashed into the office and picked up the phone to room 523, a hoarse male voice picked up, "The garage. Now."

"Yes boss." He drawled and hung up.

I could hear the roar of the engine outside, and I rushed towards the waiting car. Thoughts of Mia dissipated like smoke to the back of my mind.

Fucking room 523. I had hoped to never have to call it again. I gritted my teeth and had barely closed the door when Salvatore took off.

He tore down the road, paying no attention to the other traffic—screeching tyres spinning and screaming on the tar.

We swallowed our words and hid behind the silence of our thoughts. Lupe had been a distraction, Mia was a worse one. Lupe was a free agent. He would be for hire to the highest bidder. His masters had cut him loose, but not before they took their pound of flesh. And whatever he had sold himself to, was not paying him enough—not enough to even pretend like he was getting paid. It begged the question, what did he ask for as payment. As the thoughts niggled and bit into my brain, we pulled up to the garage.

My raging heart sighed in relief as I saw the building still standing. I stumbled out of the car and ran towards it. I've only been away a few weeks but it already felt like a lifetime had gone by. Salvatore ran over to Lorenzo who's nose dripped like a tap. Red blotches exploding at his feet. Like the other's, he'd been beaten badly.

I smashed through the iron door, knowing there was no one left to find. I should have cancelled the call to 523. But maybe it was time to utilise my dark, little secret. They would be here in a matter of minutes anyway.

I stepped inside and my heart stalled. The place had been ransacked, systematically destroyed. My eyes swept across it as I took in the damage.

The floor sparkled, a shower of broken glass covered it like it had been swept by a mid-afternoon hail storm. Every car in the garage had been beaten and dented, tyres punctures, paint scratched, and windows shattered.

I edged inside. The kitchenette had been destroyed, the table up turned, and chairs smashed. Every cupboard was open, hanging on hinges, the contents crudely spilt onto the floor. My lips curled and my hand shook at my sides, my fists pumping. All my muscles straining and taut.

I pushed through the door to my room. Like the rest of

the place, it had been destroyed. But my eyes were drawn to the wall where they had left a message smeared in blood.

"I will take everything from you."

I sucked in the heavy air around me, toxic with anger and hate. I swivelled around when I heard footsteps. Salvatore stood at the door, his eyes narrowed as he read the message.

"The boys are here."

I nodded and took a final glance back over the writing. If he wanted a war, I was about to give him one.

The men crammed into the room, a pool of testosterone and muscle all rubbed against one another. Clad in black and heavily armed, my army gathered before me.

Room 523.

The one secret I kept from Mia, from the world—an army of loyal soldiers I had amassed over time. Men so broken, even after they helped me destroy the men's lives that night when we burned all those men, they could not be released back into society.

These were the faulty and abused, the dogs hurt so deeply that the anger and aggression became a part of who they were. If I was to set them loose, only pain and death would ensue. So I kept them on the fortieth floor for the last ten years. Every whim has been catered to—money, food, women. All they had to do was stay ready and stay prepared, in case one day I would need their services again. It seemed that the day had come.

Dalton walked towards me, a giant of a man. His massive shoulders strapped with weapons, his shaved head peppered with blond flakes of re growth, "Boss, so nice to hear your voice again."

I wished I felt the same as I tipped my head and shook his hand. "How can we help?" His gaze swept the room, we both knew they had come too late.

"I want you to clean up," he waited in silence as I elaborated, "I want these cars gone and this place swept—the builders will come tonight to fix what needs fixing and the cars will be replaced."

Dalton crossed his arms across his chest, waiting for more. We both knew I didn't him call out there to clean my fucking workshop.

"And then, I want you to clean up. Anyone left alive needs to disappear."

Salvatore shot me a look, but I continued before he could say anything, "Males only, and keep it quiet and swift. I want it done by the end of tomorrow."

"So be it." Dalton gathered his men around him. I didn't look behind me as I stepped back outside.

"You're hunting the wrong people. We already broke them, they would never—"

"How do you know? It's been almost a fucking year since this fucker started his games, since he sent his first message, and we've been chasing our fucking tail!" I screamed at him, "Mia, Simone, the boys…What next? I'm not taking any more chances. I'm going to flush that fucker out.

"You're not thinking straight, you're distracted."

"Fuck you!"

"Fuck me?" He pushed me, "Closing down Sin so your girlfriend can dance dirty for you? Sending Dalton out on a witch hunt? Los—"

Before he could continue, I swung at him. He dodged my fist and threw me a disgusted look. He walked to the car and slammed the door behind him looking ahead at the road. The engine roared to life as he sat idle, waiting for me.

I scrubbed my hands over my face and grimaced. He was right. But I didn't care.

I slammed the door behind me as I slid into the seat.

"Dalton and his boys will go, that's not negotiable. We do have one more avenue though."

He nodded and took off, ignoring me all the way to Hill Street.

PART XXII

"Pack your bags Mia, we're going."

"Where are we going Gabriel?"

"Away."

"Where?"

I grabbed her face, my fingers digging into her cheeks, making her mouth pout. She fought against my touch, but I locked her in.

"Stop asking questions Mia, and do what you're told." I released her and she stepped back.

"Gabriel, what's going on?"

So.Fucking.Stubborn.

Maybe I should have fucked her into submission. I set the thought aside for later. Maybe Mia just needed to be broken like a wild horse. But then she wouldn't be Mia. I sucked in a galvanising breath.

"You wanted a war Mia. Now it's at my doorstep, and I will not lose anyone else."

"So we're running away?"

I gritted my teeth and fought my body, my palm burning with a desire to slap her across her face and make her see clearly.

"You think I want to leave? I've already had to leave my home to come and live here, now you've given me no other option but to get away.

"Gabriel—"

"No! I want you to be safe. Salvatore can handle things from this end, you've already interfered too much, and I can't think clearly if I think you're unsafe."

"Gabriel—"

"Mia!" I sucked in a deep breath and wrenched my hands through my hair, "Please. Just do this one thing for me."

She nodded silently and opened up her drawers.

As we rode down the elevator, I replayed the conversation I had with Salvatore earlier.

"You need to leave and take her with you."

"What are you talking about?"

"You know I'm right." He leaned against the office desk, his hands gripping the lip.

I gritted my teeth and cocked my head. There was no arguing; ever since Mia had come into my life the delicate balance I had achieved had been turned on its head. She'd pried too many secrets from me and had my head in all the wrong place.

Salvatore's hand landed on my shoulder as my thoughts evaporated, "It's ok little brother, it's happened to the best of us."

"Not to you."

"Well..." his eyes shot to the door and back to me, "Guess not."

"I can fire her." His eyes shot to my face. "You can look after her. You have almost as much money as I do." The tip of my lip tilted at the thought.

He didn't answer, "Go upstairs, pack your bags. Paperwork was drawn up a week ago, it's basically yours."

I gave him a long lingering look. "Stop it." He said and moved around the desk falling into the chair. "I've got it. Let's be honest, you haven't really been interested in this place since opening night."

He was right.

"Go. Get Mia somewhere safe and I'll come get you in the morning for our scheduled visit."

"Salvatore—"I started.

"I know."

W e climbed on the bike, the chilly air already piercing our skin. It was going to be a hard ride, but maybe that's how all new beginnings need to start. Crisp and hard and frozen along the surface, until it begins to thaw and crack and become something softer. A life we could sink right into.

I don't know if it was my tone or the look I gave her before we left, but Mia didn't argue. She didn't fight. She climbed onto the bike and held onto me. Her grip tight and fierce.

Maybe I should have seen it then. Felt it.

We drove into the dark night, the tall tower of Hill Street dimming behind us until it was nothing but a few glowing lights in the distance—unrecognisable.

The bike roared beneath us, between us, and inside us.

As we turned onto the side road, I felt Mia stiffen behind me, her hands digging it to me. I drove below the tree canopy and exited on the other side, pulling up to the main house.

I turned the ignition off and the silence enveloped us as quickly as the dark. Mia climbed off and pulled off her helmet, looking at the house.

"What are we doing here Gabriel?"

"This is our new home." I brushed a hand through my hair, despite the cold sweat covering my forehead.

"What are you talking about?" She seemed hesitant.

"You said you loved it here when we came to visit."

"I did, but—"

"So, I bought it for you."

"Gabriel?"

"This is the life that was stolen from you, the life you loved. Now I have a chance to give you everything you wanted."

She gasped, her hand covered that space where her heart lived. She looked at my face, a tortured expression covered hers as she whispered, "Gabriel I already have everything I could possibly want."

"Well now you have more."

"I don't want it, or this. I just want us."

"We can't have an *us* at Hill Street, and you deserve better than the garage, better than a one bedroom hole that smells like grease and petrol."

"It smells like you."

"Spots loves it here, he has space to run and explore—to be a dog."

"Gabriel."

On cue, Spots ran at me from the darkness. His happy bark echoing in the deep night as he bounded towards us, his tail wagging and his breath steaming from his mouth.

"Hey buddy, do you like it here?" I scratched his ear and he barked again.

A faint light grew closer and Spots' bark changed. He growled and his teeth shone in the torch light as he bared them.

"Just me here," Geoffrey's voice came from the path and soon he was standing before us. His features blurred in the dim moonlight, the torch lighting only the tar below our feet, "Just came to see you made it here all right and you're all settled."

"We're fine." His eyes met mine and we stood there for a minute, two males assessing the other, encroaching on one another's territory.

"Right then. Good night. I'll see you in the morning."

"No you won't."

"Excuse me?"

"I've kept you on to run this farm for me. I have no desire to be up with the sun or before it."

"I see," I could almost taste the distain in his voice The city boy that had no desire to be a cowboy. "Suit yourself." He turned around and walked away, the light of his torch fading as he rounded a corner.

Spots stood back up, his nose to the ground, his tail wagging.

"You kept him on?" Mia's voice held a note that took me a minute to decipher, one I'd not heard there before.

She was scared.

"Just for a while, till we get settled. Then, this place will be yours to run, hire whoever you want, fire everyone—I don't care, as long as you're happy."

Spots barked again and crisp wind tore through us.

"Let's get inside."

"Gabriel," Mia grabbed my arm as I unlocked the front door. I turned to her, "I don't like him."

"It'll be ok."

"I want him gone." She stood on the threshold, mouth chattering, arms folded across her body holding in whatever warmth they could afford her.

"In the morning, first thing. I promise."

She flashed me a smile that wasn't entirely happy, more like relieved.

We walked into the farmhouse—large wooden beams and high ceilings, polished floors, and not much else.

Mia's eyes swept the near empty space.

"There's a bed upstairs already made. The rest you can choose, make this house our home. This is a clean slate, not a trace of history. Nothing here tells a story. Once we make this a house, we can make it our own."

I slipped a hand around Mia's shoulder and took her around the massive five-bedroom house. Whatever the future held, this place would be big enough to accommodate for it.

Or so I thought.

Mia seemed subdued, lost somewhere. That far away look back in her eyes. I led her upstairs and into the master bedroom.

"Are you ok Mia?"

She nodded but her glazed eyes and drawn expression pinched my heart.

"I need to tell you something." She looked at her hands, her fingers lacing in and out of one another.

"In the morning, luce mia. We have plenty of time."

Except that we didn't, and I should have listened.

I slept like shit. Mia tossed and turned beside me all night. I stretched and went for a piss, leaving Mia to sleep. I grabbed a pair of jeans and went downstairs to the kitchen and made a coffee. The house glowed with the sun as it kissed the wooden panels, making it seem like the entire house was coated in gold.

Spots scampered up to me, his nails scratching on the wooden floors.

"Hey buddy. You wanna go for a walk?"

He barked his response.

"Shhh, Mia is sleeping."

He barked again at the mention of her name, and I rolled my eyes leading him to the door. The morning air smacked my skin and burned my face. I pulled on a jacket and boots while Spots ran up and down the path, waiting for me.

In the sunlight everything seemed bigger like it had taken a deep breath and expanded. The farm seemed to stretch on forever as I scanned it from the front porch. Everything was just so open, so peaceful. Isolation suddenly felt very vulnerable.

I followed Spots as he ran, marking every bush and tree, every shrub and rock. He leapt and bounded, exploring the farm through his senses. He would be happy here, we all would.

When we came back, Mia was up and draped in one of my shirts. She looked sexy as hell bending over the kitchen island and sipping on her coffee.

"Hey."

"Hi." She flashed me a smile.

"Did you sleep well?"

She shrugged, "I'll sleep better once you get rid of that Geoffrey guy and his crew."

I kissed her, a tender soft peck on her lips, "This morning, right after breakfast."

But before I finished my promise the phone rang.

"Morning boss."

"What do you want?"

"Just checking that you're still running on time? We're heading out now."

Fuck. I raked a hand through my hair and my gaze flickered to Mia. She isn't going to like this, "Yup, I'll head out in ten."

Mia's eyes shot to mine. The line went dead.

"Head out where?"

"I have to go meet Salvatore."

"But we just got here. You promised to get rid Geoffrey, and that we would go shopping and talk." Her hands were on her hips, her fingers turning white.

I sighed, looking up to the ceiling, "I know. I know I promised, and I can promise you that Geoffrey will be gone by the end of the day. I just *have* to go meet Salvatore now."

"Why?"

"Mia—"

"Why? Why is he more important than I am?"

"That's not fair."

"It's not!" She pouted.

I was on her in two steps. My hands wrapped around her, and I pulled her close to me, her heat searing my skin. I kissed her forehead and leaned into her so that our foreheads touched.

"It's the first lead we've had to finding this man, and it might be the last. I *have* to go Mia."

Her mouth stretched and her brows gathered.

"It'll be a couple of hours, tops." I pulled away from her and grabbed my bike keys, and helmet.

"Gabriel…"

"I know." I said as I stepped outside and closed the door behind me.

Problem was, I didn't know anything.

PART XXIII

The door creaked like the moaning of a dying old man as we pulled on it. It dug into the gravel, tilting slightly off the old hinges. It hung unbalanced—just like we were all about to be. The smell hit us first. The stink of what was probably human feces coated the air. It crawled deep into my nostrils and down my throat, and made me want to gag.

The open door drew a strip of white light into the dark room, and in the corner we found the creature. It was decaying, starving, and wasting away into nothingness. Because he too was nothing, and he needed to remember that.

He flinched at the sound of the door and covered his eyes at the too bright light. Light. He would be starved of that too. He cowered in the corner, gradually letting his hand fall from his face, his eyes blinking until he could focus. His brown eyes held my own, glaring and burning.

I recognised hate when I saw it. I have no doubt he saw the same look in mine. He shuffled against the wall, trying to make himself smaller like he wanted to disappear. But there would be no time for that today.

I took another step into the room, the stench overwhelming. I signalled to Romeo who begrudgingly reached for the

overflowing bucket and stepped outside. It made little difference, the smell of shit and desperation clung to the walls.

"Stefano," I started. The small gaunt man turned his head
in my direction and snarled. He was half the man he used to
be, but just as alive as ever.

"Did you miss me?" I prodded. His upper lip curled in
disgust, and he looked away at his bony hands, long skeletal
fingers scratched an oozing sore on his neck.

"Do you like your accommodation?" Still he ignored me,
his fingers tracing his pointy body, now all edges and
protruding bone.

"I wish I could have come sooner, but there's been some
trouble," at that he grinned, satisfied, "I do hope this time
alone gave you some time to think."

"Fuck you." His voice croaked and grated like it had just
woken up from a long sleep.

"You know what? It's hard to talk in all this stink," he
went back to ignoring me, "I think it's time for a shower." At
that he looked up as me, his eyes wide. I stepped aside
allowing Salvatore to step forward with a hose. He flashed
Stephano a smile before he released the blast of water.

The water smashed against his naked form that was
nothing more but a skeleton covered in loose, sickly skin. He
screamed and wailed as the water rushed along his infected
body, washing always piss and ooze, searing his senses with
cold. The water pooled on the concrete floor and streamed
towards us, running outside like a putrid lake. Everything
that touched Stephano turned to shit.

He gurgled and choked as the water splashed across his
face, driving him into the wall. His feeble attempts to cover
his face were useless against the powerful force of the water.

I wanted to feel sorry for him but, truth be told, I felt
nothing. I wondered what Mia would think if she knew of
this, of this hidden side of me—a side I never wanted to show
her. I brushed the thought away.

Stephano turned his back to us, the water slicing along his skin. His howls echoing in the small, concrete cave.

"Stop!" He screamed and gurgled, "Stop. Please stop."

I let Salvatore go on for another minute and then gave him the signal to turn off the hose. Stephano looked like a drowned cat, pathetic and dripping. His long hair clumped over his eyes and plastered to his neck, his eyes scathing.

"You smell better."

"Fuck you." He hissed.

"Have you been enjoying your stay Stephano? I hear the food could be better."

"Fuck you," he sneered, "I know why you're here." His smile grew wider, "You still haven't found anything and you need my help." I could see the thought gave him immense pleasure.

"Do I?"

"Why else would you be here? Why else would you have kept me alive all this time? You need something and you think I'm gonna help you," he spat out the last, "But I've got news for you, you piece of shit, I'm not gonna give you anything. You'll never get anything out of me."

"Are you sure about that? Would you like to spend another six months in here and think about it?" His eyes widened for a second then his face dropped to his feet.

"Fuck you D'Angelo."

I shrugged, "Good seeing you Stephano." I turned my back to him and took a step towards the exit.

"Wait. Wait. Wait! Wait!" I didn't stop, "Gabriel, wait," he was begging, breaking. This is what I needed. "Maybe we can talk."

I turned back towards him not stepping any closer.

"What you do want to talk about?"

He shrugged, "I don't suppose you have a cigarette on you?"

"No, but he might." I turned towards Salvatore who

produced a box of cigarettes. Tormentingly slow, he unwrapped the plastic cover and pulled out a single cigarette. Stephano's eyes didn't leave Salvatore's hand. He licked his lips, his eye growing wider

Salvatore held the cigarette out, "You're gonna have to come here if you want it. I'm not going to step in your shit."

Stephano shuffled towards us until the slack in his chain grew taught and he couldn't come any closer. His entire body leaned and stretched towards Salvatore who waited. Stephano looked broken, but his mind was still working hard. I could see his eyes flicker to the open door, to the dim winter sunlight, to the fresh air that waited outside.

Salvatore placed the cigarette in his mouth and it fell into the water below. Stephano's face cracked. Salvatore pulled out a second cigarette and when he placed it in Stephano's mouth he grabbed it with his teeth and waited. He was like a dog, a broken, pathetic dog. But every dog had a wild streak and Stephano was no exception.

Salvatore lit a match that hissed in the small room and held it to the end of Stephano's cigarette. He inhaled deeply and took a few steps back so that he could place it between his fingers, "Thank you, thank you." He sucked on the cigarette. Blue and white smoke filled the space, suffocating us. The stench of shit mingled with the heavy reek of smoke.

"How can I help you Gabriel?" He looked at the cigarette in his hand as if it was a natural extension of his body.

"Emilio Rocco."

His eyes shot to mine and he held my gaze, "You still haven't figured it out have you? You still don't know who he is." The mocking sneer crossed his face again, and I pushed my hands into my pockets clenching my fists. For now, I still needed the fucker.

"No more games Stephano. Talk."

"People will be looking for me."

I laughed, "It's been months Stephano. No one's been

looking for you, nobody gives a shit that you've disappeared off the face of the planet. Your boys have moved on, everyone thinks you're dead."

His face creased as he thought and inhaled, blue smoke flowing from his mouth.

"Tell me what you know."

"Why? You're gonna kill me anyway."

"Maybe I'll set you free. Or maybe I'll walk out of this room and never come back. Not me, not anyone. You think one meal a day and a clean bucket is hard? I will leave you here to rot. No one will ever know that you ever existed. There will be no more food, no water, no light, no contact. You will die screaming in darkness, covered in your own shit."

"How can I trust you."

"Does it matter?"

He sucked on his cigarette, the ember burning orange as it burned the butt. He looked at it longingly and threw it on the floor. It hissed as it touched the pooled water. He shivered and pushed a wet lock of hair away from his eyes.

"Why don't you quit stalling and just tell me what you know."

"I don't know a lot, but I know someone who knows everything. Your problem has been that you've been looking in all the wrong places. You've been looking over your shoulder and in the countryside, I bet you've even been looking in those videotapes."

I didn't respond, my heart chugging in my chest. I could hear it too loudly in this tomb.

"Where you should have been looking is closer to home." A smile split his face and it wasn't mocking, it was pure joy.

"What are you talking about? Close to home?"

"I'm talking about his daughter, the one you've been fucking for the last year." His cackles echoed in the small chamber, a maniacal laugh that distorted his face. My heart slammed in my chest as I digested his words.

"Say that again…slowly." I hissed through gritted teeth.

"Mia Ritzzi is Emilio Rocco's daughter. If you want to know where he is, just ask her." His laughter grew.

I gritted my teeth, pretending my entire insides were not collapsing, that my heart was not smashing against my ribs trying to break itself open. *Mia.*

I turned to Salvatore, "I think Stephano here needs another shower before we go."

We stepped outside, Salvatore's hand landing on my shoulder. "Don't do anything rash, wait for me."

I tipped my head raking a hand through my hair.

Salvatore said nothing else. He grabbed the hose and returned to the door. The water drowned out Stephano's laughter, pushing him against the wall as he clawed against the deluge. I could hear his gurgled screams as I walked away.

"D'Angelo, set me free! You promised!"

I sucked in fresh air. My throat threatening to close. I grabbed my helmet and climbed on my bike, the engine screaming to life.

I tore down the road towards the farm wondering who the fuck was Mia Ritzzi.

To be continued...

ACKNOWLEDGMENTS

A Word from Jane:

I would like to start by thanking you, the reader, so much for reading! If you enjoyed the story, please leave a review and recommend the book to any friend you think would love Gabriel's story. You will have my eternal love and gratitude. Even a few short words go a long way.

As always, I would love to thank my wonderful friend and beta, Dawn. Her enthusiasm knows no boundaries, her genuine love for books, reading, and helping authors is contagious and humbling. I have loved having her in my corner. Thank you.

To all my other betas and C/Ps, your input and critiques have been invaluable. Without you, Gabriel would not be where he is today.

ABOUT THE AUTHOR

ABOUT THE AUTHOR

Jane Wynters doesn't quite know how to answer the question of "where are you from?" She's moved from place to place like a snowflake on the wind always searching for a safe place to land. She loves meeting new people and exploring new places. She loves reading, writing and conjuring new worlds from her imagination. Coffee is at the top of her food pyramid and she is fluent in three languages, her favourite being sarcasm.

Want to know more about the author and keep in touch? Get snippets of upcoming books and have a bit of twisted fun?

Come join me in Wonderland.